This book is the third in Harper & Row's Native American Publishing Program. All profits from this Program will be set aside in a special fund and used to support special projects designed to aid the Native American people.

# Winter
# in the
# Blood

# Winter in the Blood

## JAMES WELCH

**HARPER & ROW, PUBLISHERS**
New York    Evanston    San Francisco    London

WINTER IN THE BLOOD

Grateful acknowledgement is made to the *South Dakota
Review* in which a portion of this work first appeared.

Library of Congress Cataloging in Publication Data
Welch, James, 1940–
Winter in the blood.
I.  Title.
PZ4.W439Wi  [PS3573.E44]     813'.5'4     74–5985
ISBN 0–06–451990–2

*First Edition*

**For My Mother
and Father**

Bones should never tell a story
to a bad beginner. I ride
romantic to those words,
those foolish claims that he
was better than dirt, or rain
that bleached his cabin
white as bone. Scattered in the wind
Earthboy calls me from my dream:
Dirt is where the dreams must end.

# Part One

## 1

In the tall weeds of the borrow pit, I took a leak and watched the sorrel mare, her colt beside her, walk through burnt grass to the shady side of the log-and-mud cabin. It was called the Earthboy place, although no one by that name (or any other) had lived in it for twenty years. The roof had fallen in and the mud between the logs had fallen out in chunks, leaving a bare gray skeleton, home only to mice and insects. Tumbleweeds, stark as bone, rocked in a hot wind against the west wall. On the hill behind the cabin, a rectangle of barbed wire held the graves of all the Earthboys, except for a daughter who had married a man from Lodgepole. She could be anywhere, but the Earthboys were gone.

The fence hummed in the sun behind my back as I

climbed up to the highway. My right eye was swollen up, but I couldn't remember how or why, just the white man, loose with his wife and buying drinks, his raging tongue a flame above the music and my eyes. She was wild, from Rocky Boy. He was white. He swore at his money, at her breasts, at my hair.

Coming home was not easy anymore. It was never a cinch, but it had become a torture. My throat ached, my bad knee ached and my head ached in the even heat.

The mare and her colt were out of sight behind the cabin. Beyond the graveyard and the prairie hills, the Little Rockies looked black and furry in the heat haze.

Coming home to a mother and an old lady who was my grandmother. And the girl who was thought to be my wife. But she didn't really count. For that matter none of them counted; not one meant anything to me. And for no reason. I felt no hatred, no love, no guilt, no conscience, nothing but a distance that had grown through the years.

It could have been the country, the burnt prairie beneath a blazing sun, the pale green of the Milk River valley, the milky waters of the river, the sagebrush and cottonwoods, the dry, cracked gumbo flats. The country had created a distance as deep as it was empty, and the people accepted and treated each other with distance.

But the distance I felt came not from country or people; it came from within me. I was as distant from myself as a hawk from the moon. And that was why I had no particular feelings toward my mother and grandmother. Or the girl who had come to live with me.

I dropped down on the other side of the highway, slid through the barbed-wire fence and began the last two miles home. My throat ached with a terrible thirst.

## 2

"She left three days ago, just after you went to town."

"It doesn't matter," I said.

"She took your gun and electric razor."

The room was bright. Although it was early afternoon, the kitchen light was burning.

"What did you expect me to do? I have your grandmother to look after, I have no strength, and she is young—Cree!"

"Don't worry," I said.

"At least get your gun back." My mother swept potato peels off the counter into a paper sack at her feet. "You know she'd sell it for a drink."

The gun, an old .30–30, had once been important to me. Like my father before me, I had killed plenty of deer with it, but I hadn't used it since the day I killed Buster Cutfinger's dog for no reason except that I was drunk and it was moving. That was four years ago.

I heard a clucking in the living room. The rocking chair squeaked twice and was silent.

"How is she?" I asked.

"Hot cereal and pudding—how would you expect her to be?"

"What, no radishes?"

My mother ignored me as she sliced the potatoes into thin wafers.

"Why don't we butcher one of those heifers? She could eat steak for the rest of her life and then some."

"She'll be gone soon enough without you rushing

3

things. Here, put this on that eye—it'll draw out the poison." She handed me a slice of potato.

"How's Lame Bull?"

She stopped slicing. "What do you mean by that?"

"How's Lame Bull?"

"He'll be here this evening; you can find out then. Now get me another bucket of water."

"How's the water?" I asked.

"It'll do. It never rains anymore." She dumped the slices into a pan. "It never rains around here when you need it."

I thought how warm and flat the water would taste. No rain since mid-June and the tarred barrels under the eaves of the house were empty. The cistern would be low and the water silty.

A fly buzzed into the house as I opened the door. The yard was patched with weeds and foxtail, sagebrush beyond the fence. The earth crumbled into powder under my feet; beneath the sun which settled into afternoon heat over the slough, two pintail ducks beat frantically above the cottonwoods and out of sight. As I lowered the bucket into the cistern, a meadowlark sang from the shade behind the house. The rope was crusty in my hands. Twice I lifted and dropped the bucket, watching the water flow in over the lip until the bucket grew heavy enough to sink.

The girl was no matter. She was a Cree from Havre, scorned by the reservation people. I had brought her home with me three weeks ago. My mother thought we were married and treated her with politeness. My mother was a Catholic and sprinkled holy water in the corners of her house before lightning storms. She drank with the priest from Harlem, a round man with distant eyes, who refused to set foot on the reservation. He never buried Indians in their family graveyards; instead, he made them come to him, to his church, his saints and holy water, his feuding eyes. My mother drank with him in his shingle house beside the yellow plaster church. She thought I had married the girl and tried to welcome her, and the girl sat sullen in the living room across from the old lady, my grandmother, who filled her stone pipe with cuts of tobacco mixed with dried crushed chokecherries. She sat across from the girl, and the girl read movie magazines and imagined that she looked like Raquel Welch.

The old lady imagined that the girl was Cree and enemy and plotted ways to slit her throat. One day the flint striker would do; another day she favored the paring knife she kept hidden in her legging. Day after day, these two sat across from each other until the pile of movie magazines spread halfway across the room and the paring knife grew heavy in the old lady's eyes.

## 3

I slid down the riverbank behind the house. After a half-hour search in the heat of the granary, I had found a red and white spoon in my father's toolbox. The treble hook was rusty and the paint on the spoon flecked with rust. I cast across the water just short of the opposite bank. There was almost no current. As I retrieved the lure, three mallards whirred across my line of vision and were gone upriver.

The sugar beet factory up by Chinook had died

seven years before. Everybody had thought the factory caused the river to be milky but the water never cleared. The white men from the fish department came in their green trucks and stocked the river with pike. They were enthusiastic and dumped thousands of pike of all sizes into the river. But the river ignored the fish and the fish ignored the river; they refused even to die there. They simply vanished. The white men made tests; they stuck electric rods into the water; they scraped muck from the bottom; they even collected bugs from the fields next to the river; they dumped other kinds of fish in the river. Nothing worked. The fish disappeared. Then the men from the fish department disappeared, and the Indians put away their new fishing poles. But every now and then, a report would trickle down the valley that someone, an irrigator perhaps, had seen an ash-colored swirl suck in a muskrat, and out would come the fishing gear. Nobody ever caught one of these swirls, but it was always worth a try.

I cast the spoon again, this time retrieving faster.

The toolbox had held my father's tools and it was said in those days that he could fix anything made of iron. He overhauled machinery in the fall. It was said that when the leaves turned, First Raise's yard was full of iron; when they fell, the yard was full of leaves. He drank with the white men of Dodson. Not a quiet man, he told them stories and made them laugh. He charged them plenty for fixing their machines. Twenty dollars to kick a baler awake—one dollar for the kick and nineteen for knowing where to kick. He made them laugh until the thirty-below morning ten years ago we found him sleeping in the borrow pit across from Earthboy's place.

He had had dreams. Every fall, before the first cold wind, he dreamed of taking elk in Glacier Park. He planned. He figured out the mileage and the time it would take him to reach the park, and the time it would take to kill an elk and drag it back across the boundary to his waiting pickup. He made a list of food and supplies. He inquired around, trying to find out what the penalty would be if they caught him. He wasn't crafty like Lame Bull or the white men of Dodson, so he had to know the penalty, almost as though the penalty would be the inevitable result of his hunt.

He never got caught because he never made the trip. The dream, the planning and preparation were all part of a ritual—something to be done when the haying was over and the cattle brought down from the hills. In the evening, as he oiled his .30–30, he explained that it was better to shoot a cow elk because the bulls were tough and stringy. He had everything figured out, but he never made the trip.

My lure caught a windfall trunk and the brittle nylon line snapped. A magpie squawked from deep in the woods on the other side of the river.

## 4

"Ho, you are fishing, I see. Any good bites?" Lame Bull skittered down the bank amid swirls of dust. He stopped just short of the water.

"I lost my lure," I said.

"You should try bacon," he said, watching my line float limp on the surface. "I know these fish."

It was getting on toward evening. A mosquito lit on Lame Bull's face. I brought in the line and tied it to the reel handle. The calf bawled in the corral. Its mother, an old roan with one wild eye, answered from somewhere in the bend of the horseshoe slough.

"You should try bacon. First you cook it, then dump the grease into the river. First cast, you'll catch a good one."

"Are the fish any good?" I asked.

"Muddy. The flesh is not firm. It's been a poor season." He swatted a cloud of dust from his rump. "I haven't seen such a poor year since the flood. Ask your mother. She'll tell you."

We climbed the bank and started for the house. I remembered the flood. Almost twelve years ago, the whole valley from Chinook on down was under water. We moved up to the agency and stayed in an empty garage. They gave us typhoid shots.

"You, of course, are too young."

"I was almost twenty," I said.

"Your old man tried to ride in from the highway but his horse was shy of water. You were not much more than a baby in Teresa's arms. His horse threw him about halfway in."

"I remember that. I was almost twenty."

"Ho." Lame Bull laughed. "You were not much more than a gleam in your old man's eye."

"His stirrup broke—that's how come the horse threw him. I saw his saddle. It was a weakness in the leather."

"Ho."

"He could outride you any day."

"Ho."

Lame Bull filled the width of the doorframe as he

entered the kitchen. He wasn't tall, but broad as a bull from shoulders to butt.

"Ah, Teresa! Your son tells me you are ready to marry me."

"My son tells lies that would make a weasel think twice. He was cut from the same mold as you." Her voice was clear and bitter.

"But why not? We could make music in the sack. We could make those old sheets sing."

"Fool . . . you talk as though my mother had no ears," Teresa said.

Two squeaks came from the living room.

"Old woman! How goes the rocking?" Lame Bull moved past my mother to the living room. "Do you make hay yet?"

The rocking chair squeaked again.

"She has gone to seed," I said. "There is no fertilizer in her bones."

"I seem to find myself surrounded by fools today." Teresa turned on the burner beneath the pan filled with potatoes. "Maybe one of you fools could bring yourself to feed that calf. He'll be bawling all night."

Evening now and the sky had changed to pink reflected off the high western clouds. A pheasant gabbled from a field to the south. A lone cock, he would be stepping from the wild rose along an irrigation ditch to the sweet alfalfa field, perhaps to graze with other cocks and hens, perhaps alone. It is difficult to tell what cocks will do when they grow old. They are like men, full of twists.

The calf was snugged against the fence, its head between the poles, sucking its mother.

"Hi! Get out of here, you bitch!"

She jumped straight back from the fence, skittered sideways a few feet, then stood, tensed. Her tongue hung a thread of saliva almost to the ground and the one wild eye, rimmed white, looked nowhere in particular.

"Don't you know we're trying to wean this fool?"

I moved slowly toward the calf, backing it into a corner where the horse shed met the corral fence, talking to it, holding out my hand. Before it could move I grabbed it by the ear and whirled around so that I could pin its shoulder against the fence. I slapped a mosquito from my face and the calf bawled; then it was silent.

Feeling the firmness of its thigh, I remembered how my brother, Mose, and I used to ride calves, holding them for each other, buckling on the old chaps we found hanging in the horse shed, then the tense "Turn him out!" and all hell busted loose. Hour after hour we rode calves until First Raise caught us.

The calf erupted under my arm, first backing up into the corner, then lunging forward, throwing me up against the horse shed. A hind hoof grazed the front of my shirt.

I pitched some hay into the corral, then filled the washtub with slough water. Tiny bugs darted through the muck. They looked like ladybugs with long hind legs. A tadpole lay motionless at the bottom of the tub. I scooped it out and laid it on a flat chunk of manure. It didn't move. I prodded it with a piece of straw. Against the rough texture of the manure it glistened like a dark teardrop. I returned it to the tub, where it drifted to the bottom with a slight wriggle of its tail.

The evening was warm and pleasant, the high pink clouds taking on a purple tint. I chased the cow back up into the bend of the slough. But she would be back. Her bag was full of milk.

## 5

After supper, my mother cleared the table. Lame Bull finished his coffee and stood up.

"I must remember to get some more mosquito dope." Teresa emptied the last drops into the palm of her hand. She smeared it on her face and neck. "If your grandmother wants anything, you see that she gets it." She rested her hand on Lame Bull's forearm and they walked out the door.

I poured myself another cup of coffee. The sound of the pickup motor surprised me. But maybe they were going after groceries. I went into the living room.

"Old woman, do you want some music?" I leaned on the arms of her rocker, my face not more than six inches from hers.

She looked at my mouth. Her eyes were flat and filmy. From beneath the black scarf, a rim of coarse hair, parted in the middle, framed her gray face.

"Music," I commanded, louder this time.

"Ai, ai," she cackled, nodding her head, rocking just a bit under the weight of my arms.

I switched on the big wooden radio and waited for it to warm up. The glass on the face of the dial was cracked, and the dial itself was missing. A low hum filled the room. Then the music of a thousand violins. The rocking chair squeaked.

"Tobacco," I said.

The old woman looked at me.

I filled her pipe and stuck it between her lips. The kitchen match flared up, revealing the black mole on her upper lip. Three black hairs moved up and down as she sucked the smoke into her mouth.

The chair surrounded by movie magazines was uncomfortable, so I sat on the floor with my back resting against the radio. The violins vibrated through my body. The cover of the *Sports Afield* was missing and the pages were dog-eared, but I thumbed through it, looking for a story I hadn't read. I stopped at an advertisement for a fishing lure that called to fish in their own language. I tore the coupon out. Maybe that was the secret.

I had read all the stories, so I reread the one about three men in Africa who tracked a man-eating lion for four days from the scene of his latest kill—a pregnant black woman. They managed to save the baby, who, they were surprised to learn, would one day be king of the tribe. They tracked the lion's spoor until the fourth day, when they found out that he'd been tracking them all along. They were going in a giant four-day circle. It was very dangerous, said McLeod, a Pepsi dealer from Atlanta, Georgia. They killed the lion that night as he tried to rip a hole in their tent.

I looked at the pictures again. One showed McLeod and Henderson kneeling behind the dead lion; they were surrounded by a group of grinning black men. The third man, Enright, wasn't in the picture.

I looked up. The old lady was watching me.

## 6

Lame Bull and my mother were gone for three days. When they came back, he was wearing a new pair of boots, the fancy kind with walking heels, and she had on a shimmery turquoise dress. They were both sweaty and hung over. Teresa told me that they had gotten married in Malta.

That night we got drunk around the kitchen table.

## 7

Lame Bull had married 360 acres of hay land, all irrigated, leveled, some of the best land in the valley, as well as a 2000-acre grazing lease. And he had married a T-Y brand stamped high on the left ribs of every beef on the place. And, of course, he had married Teresa, my mother. At forty-seven, he was eight years younger than she, and a success. A prosperous cattleman.

The next day, Lame Bull and I were up early. He cursed as he swung the flywheel on the little John Deere. He opened up the petcock on the gas line, swung the flywheel again, and the motor chugged twice, caught its rhythm and smoothed out. We hitched the hay wagon behind the tractor and drove slowly past the corral and slough. We followed the footpath upriver, through patches of wild rose, across a field of sagebrush and down into a grove of dead white cottonwoods. A deer jumped up from its willow bed and bounded away, its white tail waving goodbye.

The cabin, log and mud, was tucked away in a bend of the river. A rusty wire ran from the only window up to the top of the roof. It was connected to a car aerial, always a mystery to me, as Lame Bull had no electricity. He gathered up his possessions—a chain saw, a portable radio, two boxes of clothes, a sheepherder's coat and the high rubber boots he wore when he irrigated.

"I must remember to get some more tire patches," he said, sticking a finger through a hole in one of the boots.

We padlocked the cabin, covered the pump with an old piece of tarp and started back, Lame Bull sniffing the sweet beautiful land that had been so good to him.

Later, as we drove past the corral, I saw the wild-eyed cow and a small calf head between the poles. The cow was licking the head. A meadowlark sang from a post above them. The morning remained cool, the sun shining from an angle above the horse shed. Behind the sliding door of the shed, bats would be hanging from the cracks.

Old Bird shuddered, standing with his hindquarters in the dark of the shed. He lifted his great white head and parted his lips. Even from such a distance I could see his yellow teeth clenched together as though he were straining to grin at us. Although he no longer worked, he still preferred the cool dark of the horse shed to the pasture up behind the slough. Perhaps he still felt important and wished to be consulted when we saddled up the red horse and Nig on those occasions when it was necessary to ride through the herd. No matter what season, what weather, he was always there.

Perhaps he felt he had as much right to this place as we had, for even now he was whinnying out a welcome. He was old and had seen most of everything.

## 8

Teresa sat on the edge of the concrete cistern.

"Your father won Amos pitching pennies at the fair. He was so drunk he couldn't even see the plates."

"Amos used to follow us out to the highway every morning," I said. "We used to have to throw rocks at him."

"The others drowned because you didn't keep the tub full of water. You boys were like that."

Her fingers, resting on her thighs, were long, the skin stretched over the bone as taut as a drumhead. We could see Lame Bull down by the granary, which doubled as a toolshed. He was sharpening a mower sickle.

"We went to town that day for groceries. I remember we went to the show."

"Yes, and when we came back, all the ducks were drowned. Except Amos. He was perched on the edge of the tub."

. "But he never went in. He must have been smarter than the others," I said.

Lame Bull's legs pumped faster. He poured some water on the spinning grindstone.

"He was lucky. One duck can't be smarter than another. They're like Indians."

"Then why didn't he go in with the other ducks?"

"Don't you remember how gray and bitter it was?"

"But the other ducks . . ."

". . . were crazy. You boys were told to keep that tub full." She said this gently, perhaps to ease my guilt, if I still felt any, or perhaps because ducks do not matter. Especially those you win at the fair in Dodson.

We had brought the ducks home in a cardboard box. There were five of them, counting Amos. We dug a hole in the ground big enough for the washtub to fit, and deep enough so that its lip would be even with the ground level. Then we filled the tub to the lip so that the ducks could climb in and out as they chose. But we hadn't counted on the ducks drinking the water and splashing it out as they ruffled their wings. That late afternoon, several days later, the water level had dropped to less than an inch below the rim of the tub. But it was enough. That one inch of galvanized steel could have been the wall of the Grand Canyon to the tiny yellow ducks.

The calf in the corral bawled suddenly.

The day the ducks drowned remained fresh in my mind. The slight smell of muskrat pelts coming from the shed, the wind blowing my straw hat away, the wind whipping the glassine window of the shed door; above, the gray slide of clouds as we stood for what seemed like hours beside the car glaring at the washtub beyond the fence. And the ducks floating with their heads deep in the water as though they searched the bottom for food. And Amos perched on the rim of the tub, looking at them with great curiosity.

My mother talked on about Amos. Not more than six feet away was the spot where the ducks had drowned.

The weeds grew more abundant there, as though their spirits had nourished the soil.

"And what happened to Amos?" I said.

"We had him for Christmas. Don't you remember what a handsome bird he was?"

"But I thought that was the turkey."

"Not at all. A bobcat got that turkey. Don't you remember how your brother found feathers all the way from the toolshed to the corral?"

"That was a hateful bird!"

"Oh." She laughed. "He used to chase you kids every time you stepped out the door. We had a baseball bat by the washstand, you remember? You kids had to take it with you every time you went to the outhouse."

"He never attacked you," I said.

"I should say not! I'd have wrung his damn neck for him."

Lame Bull sat on the wooden frame, the big gray grindstone spinning faster and faster as his legs pumped. Sparks flew from the sickle.

It was a question I had not wanted to ask: "Who . . . which one of us . . ."

Teresa read my hesitation. ". . . killed Amos? Who else? You kids had no stomach for it. You always talked big enough, Lord knows you could talk up a storm in those days, and your father . . ."

"First Raise killed him?"

"Your father wasn't even around!" Her fine bitter voice rang in the afternoon heat. "But I'll tell you one thing— I've never seen a sorrier sight when he did come back."

Now I was confused. The turkey was of little importance. I could remember his great wings crashing about my head as he dug his spurs into my sides, his weight bearing me down to the ground until I cried out. Then the yelling and the flailing baseball bat and the curses, and finally the quiet. It was always my father bending over me: "He's all right, Teresa, he's all right . . ." It was he, I thought, who had killed the turkey. But now it was my mother who had killed the turkey while First Raise was in town making the white men laugh. But he always carried me up to the house and laid me on the bed and sat with me until the burning in my head went away. Now the bobcat killed Amos . . .

"No! The bobcat killed the big turkey," she said, then added quietly, as though Lame Bull might hear over the grinding of steel, as though Bird might hear over the sound of the bawling calf, as though the fish that were never in the river might hear: "I killed Amos."

## 9

"Why did he stay away so much?" I said.

"What? Your father?" The question caught her off-guard.

"Why would he stay away so much?"

"He didn't. He was around enough. When he was around he got things accomplished."

"But you yourself said he was never around."

"You must have him mixed up with yourself. He always accomplished what he set out to do."

We were sitting on the edge of the cistern. Teresa was rubbing Mazola oil into the surface of a wooden salad bowl. It had been a gift from the priest in Harlem, but she never used it.

"Who do you think built the extra bedroom onto the house?" she said. She rubbed her glistening fingers together. "He was around enough—he was on his way home when they found him, too."

"How do you know that?" But I knew the answer.

"He was pointing toward home. They told me that."

I shook my head.

"What of it?" she demanded.

"Memory fails," I said.

It was always "they" who had found him, yet I had a memory as timeless as the blowing snow that we had found him ourselves, that we had gone searching for him after the third day, or the fourth day, or the fifth, cruising the white level of highway raised between the blue-white of the borrow pits. I could almost remember going into the bar in Dodson and being told that he had left for home the night before; so we must have been searching the borrow pits. How could we have spotted him? Was it a shoe sticking up, or a hand, or just a blue-white lump in the endless skittering whiteness? I had no memory of detail until we dug his grave, yet I was sure we had come upon him first. Winters were always timeless and without detail, but I remembered no other faces, no other voices.

My mother stood and massaged the backs of her thighs. "He was a foolish man," she said.

"Is that why he stayed away?"

"Yes, I believe that was it." She was looking toward the toolshed. Three freshly sharpened mower sickles leaned against the granary, their triangular teeth glistening like ice in the sun. "You know how it is."

19

"He wasn't satisfied," I said.

"He accomplished any number of things."

"But none of them satisfied him."

Teresa whirled around, her eyes large and dark with outrage. "And why not?"

"He wasn't happy . . ."

"Do you suppose he was happy lying in that ditch with his eyes frozen shut, stinking with beer . . ."

But that was a different figure in the ditch, not First Raise, not the man who fixed machinery, who planned his hunt with such care that he never made it. Unlike Teresa, I didn't know the man who froze in the borrow pit. Maybe that's why I felt nothing until after the funeral.

"He was satisfied," she said. "He was just restless. He could never settle down."

A sonic boom rattled the shed door, then died in the distance. Teresa looked up at the sky, her hand over her eyes. The airplane was invisible. She looked down at me. "Do you blame me?"

I scratched a mosquito bite on the back of my hand and considered.

"He was a wanderer—just like you, just like all these damned Indians." Her voice became confident and bitter again. "You I don't understand. When you went to Tacoma for that second operation, they wanted you to stay on. You could have become something."

"I don't blame you," I said.

"You're too sensitive. There's nothing wrong with being an Indian. If you can do the job, what difference does it make?"

"I stayed almost two years."

"Two years!" she said disgustedly. "One would be

more like it—and then you spent all your time up in Seattle, barhopping with those other derelicts."

"They didn't fix my knee."

"I see: it's supposed to heal by itself. You don't need to do the exercises they prescribed." She picked up the salad bowl. She was through with that part of my life. A dandelion parachute had stuck to the rim. "What about your wife?" She blew the parachute away. "Your grandmother doesn't like her."

I never expected much from Teresa and I never got it. But neither did anybody else. Maybe that's why First Raise stayed away so much. Maybe that's why he stayed in town and made the white men laugh. Despite their mocking way they respected his ability to fix things; they gave more than his wife. I wondered why he stuck it out so long. He could have moved out altogether. The ranch belonged to Teresa, so there was no danger of us starving to death. He probably stayed because of my brother, Mose, and me. We meant something to him, although he would never say it. It was apparent that he enjoyed the way we grew up and learned to do things, drive tractor, ride calves, clean rabbits and pheasants. He would never say it, though, and after Mose got killed, he never showed it. He stayed away more than ever then, a week or two at a time. Sometimes we would go after him; other times he would show up in the yard, looking ruined and fearful. After a time, a month, maybe, of feverish work, he would go off to overhaul a tractor and it would begin again. He never really stayed and he never left altogether. He was always in transit.

Ten years had passed since that winter day his wandering ended, but nothing of any consequence had happened to me. I had had my opportunity, a chance to work in the rehabilitation clinic in Tacoma. They liked me because I was smarter than practically anybody they had ever seen. That's what they said and I believed them. It took a nurse who hated Indians to tell me the truth, that they needed a grant to build another wing and I was to be the first of the male Indians they needed to employ in order to get the grant. She turned out to be my benefactor. So I came home.

"I think your grandmother deserves to be here more than your wife, don't you?"

"She's been here plenty long already," I agreed.

"Your wife wasn't happy here," Teresa said, then added: "She belongs in town."

In the bars, I thought. That's what you mean, but it's not important anymore. Just a girl I picked up and brought home, a fish for dinner, nothing more. Yet it surprised me, those nights alone, when I saw her standing in the moon by the window and I saw the moon on the tops of her breasts and the slight darkness under each rib. The memory was more real than the experience.

Lame Bull had finished his work and was walking toward us. He slapped his gloves against his thigh and looked back at the bank of glistening sickles. He seemed pleased.

"There isn't enough for you here," said my mother. "You would do well to start looking around."

## 10

Lame Bull had taken to grinning now that he was a proprietor. All day he grinned as he mowed through the fields of alfalfa and bluejoint. He grinned when he came in to lunch, and in the evening when the little tractor putted into the yard next to the granary, we could see his white teeth through the mosquito netting that hung from his hat brim. He let his whiskers grow so that the spiky hair extended down around his round face. Teresa complained about his sloppy habits, his rough face. She didn't like the way he teased the old lady, and she didn't like his habit of not emptying the dust and chaff in his pants cuffs. He grinned a silent challenge, and the summer nights came alive in the bedroom off the kitchen. Teresa must have liked his music.

We brought in the first crop, Lame Bull mowing alfalfa, snakes, bluejoint, baby rabbits, tangles of barbed wire, sometimes changing sickles four times in a single day. Early next morning he would be down by the granary sharpening the chipped, battered sickles. He insisted on both cutting and baling the hay, so my only job was the monotonous one of raking it into strips for the baler. Around and around I pulled the windrow rake, each circuit shorter than the last as I worked toward the center. I sat on the springy seat of the Farmall, which was fairly new, and watched Lame Bull in the next field. He tinkered endlessly with the baler, setting the tension tighter so that the bales would be more compact, loosening it a turn when they began to break. Occasionally I would see the tractor idling, the regular puffs of black smoke popping from its stack, and Lame Bull's legs sticking out from beneath the baler. He enjoyed being a proprietor and the haying went smoothly until we hired Raymond Long Knife to help stack bales.

Long Knife came from a long line of cowboys. Even his mother, perhaps the best of them all, rode all day, every day, when it came time to round up the cattle for branding. In the makeshift pen, she wrestled calves, castrated them, then threw the balls into the ashes of the branding fire. She made a point of eating the roasted balls while glaring at one man, then another—even her sons, who, like the rest of us, stared at the brown hills until she was done.

Perhaps it was because of this fierce mother that Long Knife had become shrewd in the way dumb men are shrewd. He had learned to give the illusion of work, even to the point of sweating as soon as he put his gloves on, while doing very little. But because he was Belva Long Knife's son and because he always seemed to be hanging around the bar in Dodson, he was in constant demand.

The day we hired him the weather changed. It was one of those rare mid-July days when the wind blows chilly through the cottonwoods and the sky seems to end fifty feet up. The ragged clouds were both a part of and apart from the grayness; streaks of white broke suddenly, allowing sun to filter through for an instant as the clouds closed and drove swiftly north.

Lame Bull of course drove the bull rake, not because he was best at it but because it was the proprietor's job. He wore his down vest and his sweat-stained pearl stetson pulled low over his big head. Although he was

thick and squat, half a head shorter than either Teresa
or I, he had a long torso; seated on the bull rake, which
was mounted on a stripped-down car frame, he looked
like a huge man, but he had to slide forward to reach
the brake and clutch pedals.

He lowered the rake and charged the first row of
bales. The teeth skimmed over the stubble, gathering in
the bales; then the proprietor pulled back a lever and
the teeth lifted. He swerved around to deliver the bales
at our feet. We began to build the stack.

By noon we had the first field cleared. Things went
smoothly enough those first two days as we moved from
field to field. Long Knife and I built the stacks well,
squaring off the corners, locking each layer in place
with the next one so that the whole wouldn't lean, or
worse, collapse. The cloudy weather held steady those
days, at times trying to clear up, at other times threatening a downpour. But the weather held and Lame Bull
was happy. He gazed lovingly at each stack we left behind us.

The third day there was not a cloud in the sky. We
didn't work that morning in order to give the bales a
chance to dry out. Although it hadn't rained, the hu-
midity and dew had dampened them just enough so that
they might spoil if we tried to stack them right away.
After lunch Long Knife and I drove out to the field in
the pickup. Lame Bull had broken two teeth on the bull
rake and screwed up the hydraulic lift, so he followed
us with the tractor and hay wagon. We would have to
pick the bales by hand, which meant a long hard afternoon. In the rearview mirror I could see Lame Bull's
grinning face, partially hidden behind the tractor's
chimney. Long Knife leaned out of the cab window and

turned his face to the sky. It was a small round face with a short sharp nose and tiny slanted eyes. They called him Chink because of those eyes. He was a tall man, slender, with just the beginnings of a paunch showing above his belt buckle. On the silver face of the buckle was a picture of a bucking horse and the words: *All-around Cowboy, Wolf Point Stampede, 1954.* The buckle was shiny and worn from scraping against the bars of taverns up and down the valley. He was not called Chink to his face because of the day he almost beat the Hutterite to death with that slashing buckle.

"Jesus, beautiful, ain't it?" he said.

I nodded, but he was still looking out the window. I said, "You bet."

"How much does Lame Bull owe me?"

"Two days—twenty bucks so far."

Long Knife continued to gaze out the window. To the north, just above the horizon, we could see the tail end of the two-day run of clouds.

"Twenty bucks—that ain't much for two days' work, is it?"

I didn't say anything.

"It's enough, though . . . By God, it's enough." He sounded as though he had made a great decision. "How much is he paying you?"

"Same thing—ten bucks a day."

"That sure ain't much." He was still leaning out the window. As he shook his head, his black hair bristled against his shirt collar.

We crossed the dry irrigation ditch. This was the last field, but the alfalfa grew thickest here and the bales were scarcely ten feet apart. I killed the motor. I could hear Long Knife's hair bristling against his collar as he continued to shake his head. We waited for Lame Bull to catch up.

He stopped the tractor beside the pickup and grinned as us as we climbed out. "You throw 'em up," he said to me. "Raymond will stack 'em—ain't it, Raymond?"

Long Knife looked uncomfortable. I could tell what was coming, but Lame Bull continued to grin. I walked over to a bale beside the wagon and threw it on. I heard Long Knife say something, but the noise of the idling tractor obscured it. I walked around the wagon and threw another bale on. Lame Bull leaned down toward Long Knife: "You what?" I threw another bale on. "You heard me!" I walked behind the wagon to the pickup. I took a drink from the water bag. "You heard me!"

Lame Bull popped the clutch on the tractor. It lurched forward and died. He stepped down and checked the hitch on the wagon. Then he walked to the front of the tractor and kicked the tire. "Remind me to put some more air in this one," he said.

Long Knife kicked one of the big rear tires and nodded. I put the cap on the water bag and hung it on the door handle. Lame Bull had his back to us. He was grinning at the field full of bales. I could tell.

"Look, you give me a ride back to town and I'll buy you a beer," Long Knife said.

I avoided his eyes. I didn't want to be his ally.

Long Knife turned to Lame Bull: "But look at my hands—they're cut and bleeding. Do you want me to get infected?"

Lame Bull refused to look at his hands. "I'll pay your doctor bills when we're through."

"My head is running in circles with this heat."

"I'll pay for your head too."

"We better get started," I said, but no one moved. I sat down on the running board.

"Look at my hands."

I looked at his hands. It was true that they were raw from throwing around the bales. One finger was actually cut.

"You did that last night on one of those movie magazines," I said. "Besides, you should have wore gloves like the rest of us."

Long Knife folded his arms and leaned against the rear fender of the pickup. It was clear that he wasn't going to work anymore, no matter what happened. We were wasting time and I wanted to get the field cleared. It was the last field.

"Listen to me, Lame Bull—let's let him go. You and me'll work twice as hard and when it's done, it's done."

My logic seemed to impress Long Knife. "Listen to him, Lame Bull."

Lame Bull didn't listen. He wasn't listening to anybody. I could tell that, as his eyes swept the field, he was counting bales, converting them into cows and the cows into calves and the calves into cash.

"You can't keep me here against my will. You have to pay me and let me go back to town."

"Listen, Lame Bull—you have to pay him," I said.

"You're damn right," Long Knife said.

"And let him go back to town."

"You tell him, boy."

"He ain't a slave, you know."

There was a pause. I could see the highway from where I sat, but there were no cars. Beyond the highway, the Little Rockies seemed even tinier than their name.

Without turning around, Lame Bull pulled out his sweaty hand-carved wallet, took out a bill, crumpled it into a ball and threw it over his head. It landed at our feet.

"That's more like it," Long Knife said, smoothing out the bill. It was a twenty. "You going to give me a ride, boy?"

"I don't have a car."

"You could take the pickup here."

"It isn't mine. It belongs to Teresa," I said.

"But she's your mother." Long Knife was getting desperate.

"She's his wife," I said, looking at Lame Bull's back. "Why don't you ask him for a ride?"

Long Knife thought about this for a minute. He pushed his hat back on his head. "I'll give you two dollars," he said, as though he had just offered Lame Bull a piece of the world. "Two dollars and a beer when we get to town."

The magpie floating light-boned through the afternoon air seemed to stop and jump straight up when Lame Bull's fist landed. Long Knife's head snapped back as he slammed into the pickup, his hat flying clear over the box. It was a sucker punch, straight from the shoulder, delievered with a jump to reach the taller man's nose.

"Jesus Christ almighty!" I said, leaping from the spray of blood.

Lame Bull was not grinning. He picked up Long Knife and threw him in the back of the pickup. "Get in," he said. I retrieved the hat—the sweatband was already wet—and climbed into the cab. Lame Bull had wrapped a blue bandanna around his hand. With shifting gears and whining motor, the pickup shot off across the fields toward the highway.

"You might have to get a tetanus shot for that hand," I said, looking through the back window at Long Knife, his face smeared with blood, his little eyes staring peacefully up at the clear blue sky.

# 11

Lame Bull didn't grin much after that; at least, not as a rule. For one thing, his hand had become infected; for another, he had decided that it was improper for a property owner to grin so much, as it just caused trouble with the hired hands, who felt they could get away with anything so long as the boss grinned.

"That's another thing the matter with these Indians." He nodded gravely.

Ferdinand Horn nodded gravely.

"They get too damn tricky for their own good."

Ferdinand Horn's wife nodded gravely.

"On the other hand, where would we be without Long Knife? He's not a bad worker and he used to be a champion—saddle bronc."

The rocking chair in the living room squeaked.

"By God, you should have seen that hat fly!" A grin flickered across Lame Bull's face.

I shook my head and grinned.

Ferdinand Horn grinned. His wife grinned. Teresa did not—she hated fighting.

"Yep." Ferdinand Horn turned to me: "I saw your woman down in Malta today."

"What woman could that be, Ferdinand?"

"What woman he says . . . no, it was her all right. She was having herself quite a time." He grinned.

"Clean over the pickup—thought his head was still in it for a minute there." Lame Bull poured himself another glass of beer from one of the quarts.

"Were her brothers around?"

"Just that one—that little guy . . ."

"Whoo! They were having some time for themselves," Ferdinand Horn's wife said. Her small brown eyes glistened behind the turquoise-frame glasses.

"Maybe I ought to go get her." I glanced at Teresa.

"Oh, she can take care of herself. At least that white man thinks so . . ." She also glanced at Teresa.

"Hell, Long Knife ain't such a bad guy," continued Lame Bull.

"The one she was riding with. They had her brother in the backseat but that didn't seem to bother them any." She took a sip of wine.

Lame Bull's hand was in a sling made from a plaid shirt. The more he drank the more the sling pulled his neck down, until he was talking to the floor. The more he talked to the floor the more he nodded. It was as though the floor were talking back to him, grave words that kept him nodding gravely. Teresa sat beside him, glaring at the bandaged hand.

"I guess I ought to go get her," I said.

"If only he'd learn to keep his mouth shut. I wouldn't have cut my knuckles up . . ."

"These days it's hard for a man to get good help," Ferdinand Horn said. "You run into these assholes who don't want to work."

His wife dabbed at her nose with a pink handkerchief,

then tucked it up her sleeve. "You should talk—with your payroll." She was impressed with Lame Bull, the property owner.

The property owner nodded to the floor.

The rocking chair squeaked three times.

"How you doing, Mama?" Teresa called into the living room.

I settled back in my chair beside the refrigerator. It was a hot day—even the flies sat heavy on the window-sills. One was wading through a puddle of wine on the table. Behind it a row of bottles glistened in the shadows of the kitchen. I scratched my knee.

"Are you going to go after her?" Teresa asked. She was wearing a pair of slacks and cowboy shirt, white anklets and sneakers. Her hair was pulled straight back from her forehead into a loose ponytail. Although never beautiful, she was a woman who had grown handsome, more so each year—First Raise had been the first to notice this trend. We were all astonished, even Teresa, but she accepted it. Her face remained unwrinkled; the skin over the bridge of her nose remained shiny and taut. Her hair was still black, almost blue in sunlight. Perhaps it was because her appearance hadn't really changed that she had become handsome. Her figure had always been stout, but it had not gone to fat. Her knuckles had not become big, though they had darkened from years of sun and garden dirt, and her fingernails were still long and fine, slightly curved over her fingertips. Perhaps it was in the eyes that she had become handsome. They seemed to grow darker, more liquid, as the years passed.

Ferdinand Horn stood up and drained his glass, then walked outside to take a leak.

Lame Bull nodded gravely to the floor.

The fly had reached the other side of the puddle of wine. First he cleaned his head with his front legs, then his wings with his back legs. He rubbed his legs together and fell over. A steady buzzing filled the room as the fly vibrated on his back. Another fly buzzed up and down the windowpane by the washbasin, then dropped to the sill. Lame Bull poured Ferdinand Horn's wife another drink. She shrieked as the wine overflowed the glass and stained the butterflies on her wrinkled print dress. She grinned at me, her eyes glittering behind the turquoise-frame glasses: "Are you going to go after her?"

I nodded gravely to the floor.

Lame Bull let out a great laugh and fell over backwards in his chair.

# 12

She was Cree and not worth a damn. Not worth going after. My grandmother, before she quit talking, had told me how Crees never cared for anybody but themselves. Crees drank too much and fought with other Indians in bars, though they had never fought on the battlefield. She told me how Crees were good only for the white men who came to slaughter Indians. Crees had served as scouts for the mounted soldiers and had learned to live like them, drink with them, and the girls had opened their thighs to the Long Knives. The children of these unions were doubly cursed in the eyes of the old woman. So she sat in the rocker and plotted ways to kill the girl who was thought to be my wife.

I lay in bed and listened to the old lady snoring in the living room. She slept in a cot beside the oil stove. Three army blankets and a star quilt covered her frail body.

Though almost a century old, almost blind and certainly toothless, she wanted to murder the girl, to avenge those many sins committed by generations of Crees. Her hands, small and black as a magpie's feet, rested limply in her lap, palms up, as she rocked the days away in the brightly lit living room—the only moving part of her her feet pushing against the floor to send the rocking chair squeaking back, then forward, and back again. If the girl had thought that her life was in danger, she would have laughed to see my mother hold the tiny body over a bedpan, to hear the small tinkling of an old lady as she sighed with relief.

This woman who was Teresa's mother had told me many things, many stories from her early life. My brother, Mose, had been alive at the time when, one winter evening as we sat at the foot of her rocker, she revealed a life we never knew, this woman who was our own kin. She told us of her husband, Standing Bear, a Blackfeet (like herself) from the plains west of here, just below the Rocky Mountains. She was a girl, barely in her teens, when Standing Bear bartered with her father, a man of some renown, a man with many scars and horses. Her husband gave her father two ponies and three robes for the young girl. The reason she came so cheap, she said, was because her father had already given away four daughters. One of these daughters was Standing Bear's second wife, so she became the third and sat between his older wives and his daughters. His sons sat on the other side of him. When guests came for meals, she sat even further away from him, but she was happy to be the wife of such a man. Sometimes she slept with him, though he was almost thirty years older than she was. On those nights, beneath the woolly robes, she snuggled against his large body and sang softly in his ear. He was good, gentle and, like her father, a chief. She sang to him.

It came as no surprise when the Long Knives rode onto the plains up near the mountains. Camps were dismantled, the tepee poles serving now as travois frames to carry supplies, furniture and old people. The dogs panted beside the horses, trying to catch what little shade the larger animals offered. Women and children walked the long sagebrush miles, in the heat, in the dust the travois kicked up, behind a small band of mounted warriors.

Fish had warned them. Fish, the medicine man. The Long Knives will be coming soon, he said, for now that the seasons change there is a smell of steel in the air. A week later the soldiers did come, but the camp was abandoned: everything had been taken and the only signs that a community had existed were the tepee rings and fireplaces and a few sticks which had been the racks that held the drying meat. It was a barren scene that greeted the soldiers.

It had been in the fall. According to our grandmother, two bands had come together at a campsite beside a snaking vein of water, flanked by stands of willow and lodgepole pines, that would become known as Little Badger. To the south, Heart Butte served as a lookout and fortress if necessary, and to the west, the great mountains with their snow caps and granite faces above the timberline.

The two bands had decided to winter together and

settled in to wait for the first wind out of the north. The days remained hot but nights came colder. Fires dotted the campsite, and in the middle, around a larger fire, men sat and talked and played stick game late into the night. A feast celebrated their coming together, and for three days the old lady, then a girl, wailed with the women around the perimeter of jogging hunters. When the men rested, she owl-danced and threw "snakes" with other girls. A dust cloud hung over the campsite until the early hours of morning.

It was on the third morning that Fish made his prophetic announcement. A week later, the scouts rode down from the butte, their horses lathered and out of breath.

When the old lady had related this story, many years ago, her eyes were not flat and filmy; they were black like a spider's belly and the small black hands drew triumphant pictures in the air.

The bands split up. Heavy Runner's group went north, following the east slope of the mountains into Canada. Standing Bear's people followed Little Badger, then Birch Creek east to the Marias River, which twisted through the hot dry plains until it turned south to enter the Missouri. They traveled east and slightly north of the morning sun until they made camp in the Bear Paw mountains. From here they made their way north to the Milk River valley, where they put in one of the hardest winters known to the old lady. Many of the band starved to death that winter. Standing Bear himself died in a futile raid on the Gros Ventres, who were also camped in the valley. When the survivors led his horse into camp, his eldest son killed it and the family lived off the meat for many days. The horse was killed because Standing Bear would need it in the other world; they ate it because they were starving.

My grandmother was not yet twenty when she became a widow. With gravity—and we had no reason to doubt her—she told us she had been a beautiful girl, slender, with flawless brown skin and long hair greased and shiny as the wing of a raven. But because she was the widow of Standing Bear, a great leader, the young men of the tribe shied away from her, and the women treated her as an outcast. She possessed a dark beauty, a gift the women envied, though they must have laughed at her willowy body's barrenness, for she had produced no children, had slept with Standing Bear only to whisper her songs.

Now the old lady snored in her cot on the other side of the wall. The house lay in the shadow of a round moon. From somewhere down the valley three or four coyotes began to bark, sharp and high-pitched like puppies. A sudden breeze made the shade flap against the window. Naked beneath a single sheet, I thought of the many nights I had lain awake, listening to those coyotes, crickets, the old lady's night sounds and my own heartbeat.

I never remembered my real grandfather's face those nights, though I was four years old when he died. The old lady never mentioned him, perhaps for fear the image of Standing Bear would die in me. For whatever reason, she remained a widow for twenty-five years before she met a half-white drifter named Doagie, who had probably built this house where now the old lady snored and I lay awake thinking that I couldn't remember his face. They lived together, this daughter of one chief, wife of another, and the half-breed drifter, though

I found out that they never married and only tolerated each other. Teresa was their only offspring. And it was questioned whether Doagie was her real father or not. The woman who had informed me made signs that he wasn't.

A low rumble interrupted my thoughts. I sat up and looked about the dark room. When I was young I had shared it with Mose and his stamp collection and his jar full of coins. In one corner against the wall stood a tall cupboard with glass doors. Its shelves held mementos of a childhood, two childhoods, two brothers, one now dead, the other servant to a memory of death. Mementos. I slipped from beneath the sheet and tiptoed to the cupboard. Two brown duck eggs lay in a nest of hay. Albums full of stamps lay beside the nest and, on a lower shelf, a rusty jackknife that we had found in an Indian grave pointed solemnly at a badger skull. Shell casings from different-caliber guns circled neatly within a larger circle of arrowheads. In the center a green metal soldier crouched, his face distorted in a grimace of anger and his rifle held high above his head.

Another rumble, closer this time, rattled the glass doors. The jar that had held the coins was still there. I picked it up and walked over to the window. In the moonlight, I could just read the message inked on a piece of adhesive tape: "Do NOT TOUCH! THIS MEANS YOU! M." I replaced the empty jar, then walked out through the living room, past the old lady's cot, through the kitchen and out the shed door. I peed on a clump of weeds beside the fence. The smell of sage was heavy in the wind. The tops of the thunderheads shone silver-white in the moon's glare. Below, the blackness was

WINTER IN THE BLOOD

rent by jagged flashes that lit up the western horizon. In the valley to the east, I could see the silhouettes of the cottonwoods that marked the curving river. The coyotes had quit barking. It was going to rain.

## 13

Lame Bull had decided the night before to give me a ride into Dodson. From there I could catch the bus down to Malta. We left early, before the gumbo flat could soak up enough rain to become impassable. The pickup slipped and skidded through the softening field as the rain beat down against the windshield. There was no wiper on my side and the landscape blurred light brown against gray. Patches of green relieved this monotony, but suddenly and without form. I had placed a piece of cardboard in my side window—the glass had fallen out one night in town last winter—to keep out the rain. I could have been riding in a submarine. At last we spun up the incline to the highway, and now I made out the straight ribbon of black through the heart of a tan land.

"Looks pretty good, huh?"

Lame Bull was referring to the rain and the effect it would have on the new growth of alfalfa.

"Not bad," I said. I didn't even want to think about haying again, not after we had struggled through that last field of bales.

"You know it." He hunched forward over the steering wheel. "I think we need a new rig, pal—the windshield wiper is slowing down on this one."

We passed Emily Short's fields, which were the best in the valley. They had been leveled by a reclamation crew from the agency. Emily was on the tribal council.

"Looky there!" Lame Bull slowed down.

Through his side window, I could see a figure in black shoveling a drain in one of the shallow irrigation ditches. A lonely moment—that man in the green field, the hills beyond and the gray sky above. His horse stood cold and miserable, one back leg cocked, the others ankle-deep in mud.

"Poor sonofabitch . . ."

When we got to Dodson, we went straight to Wally's. Lame Bull bought me a whiskey, then made out a check to me for thirty dollars. The bartender cashed it and brought another drink, including one for himself. He took the amount out of my check.

Out of habit, I decided to check for mail. As I hurried through the rain, my leg began to ache—not bad, just a dull pressure around the knee. Though it had been operated on twice, they had never managed to take away the stiffness or the ache that predicted endless dissatisfactions as surely as Teresa predicted lightning storms with her holy water.

The interior of the post office was dark and mahogany; rows of box windows reflected the gray beyond the larger gold-lettered window that looked out on the only street in town. I turned the combination dials to the numbers I had known since a child. Mose and I used to fight to see who got to open this box. There was a letter to Teresa from the priest in Harlem, a perfectly white envelope with his name stamped in silver in the corner. I started to put it back, but on second thought, more likely on no thought, I stuck it in the breast pocket of my Levi jacket. On my way out, I glanced at the men staring into the gloom of the post office from the wanted posters. They were the same faces I had memorized so many years before. Only the names were different.

I had another whiskey with Lame Bull. I thought of the hours my father had put in here, joking with the white men, the farmers from out north, the cattlemen to the east, the men from the grain elevator—they were acquaintances; they had bought me beers on those few occasions First Raise dragged me in. But they were foreign—somehow their lives seemed more orderly, they drank a lot but left early, and they would be back at work in the morning, while First Raise . . .

Now, except for the bartender and us, the place was empty. I said goodbye to Lame Bull and walked down to the café to wait for the bus. Then I walked back to the drugstore to buy a toothbrush.

## 14

The bus was two hours late. The driver, a small man with tufts of black hair sticking out his ears, took my money, then sat down to a cup of coffee. I picked up my paper sack, which contained clean underwear and socks and an extra shirt, and walked out to the bus. It had gotten noticeably darker, though it was early afternoon. I sat across from a young woman and listened to the rain drum against the roof. The driver climbed aboard, shut the door and announced that we were headed for Malta. I stared at the woman's white legs and tried to imagine what she looked like under the purple coat, but I fell asleep.

An hour later we were in Malta. I stuffed the sack up under my jacket and hurried down the street to Minough's. Dougie, my girl's brother, was sitting at the bar. Beside him a large white man dozed, his head resting on his freckled forearms. His hat was pushed back almost to his shoulders. A cigarette smoldered in the ashtray next to his curly red hair.

I set the sack on a table behind me.

"I'm looking for your sister," I said.

"How come?"

"A personal matter."

"How come?" Dougie took a comb out of his shirt pocket and blew flecks of dandruff from it. "What are you going to do when you find her?"

"That's up to her, I guess."

"You going to beat her up?" He ran the comb through his hair, fluffing the wave with his other hand.

"I don't know, maybe . . ." I tried to keep my voice down.

"What did she do to you?"

"She took some things that don't exactly belong to her," I mumbled.

He laughed. "That's her, that's the way she operates . . ." He punched me on the shoulder. "Man, you're lucky you got any nuts left—do you?" He made a sudden grab for my crotch. I flinched away. He leaned over and whispered: "See this guy here?"

"Is he the guy she's been running around with?"

"He drives a big-ass Buick."

"Where is she?"

"Help me get him back to the can and we'll see how

much money he has on him. He drives a big Buick."

"You mean he used to—she probably stole it."

"No, hell, it's parked right outside—we been riding around all day. Come on, give me a hand."

"Then you'll tell me where she is?"

"Sure."

"What if he wakes up?"

"Shit, this guy's so far gone he wouldn't know it if a cow pissed in his eye."

We dragged the big man back into the toilet. He was half a foot taller than I was. Dougie was lost under the other armpit, but he already had the man's wallet in his hand. We sat him down on the toilet.

"How much is in the wallet?" I said.

"Nothing. The sonofabitch is empty."

But I saw Dougie's small hand sneak a wad of bills into his pocket.

"Wait a minute—give me some of that."

"Bullshit. The deal was I was just going to tell you where my sister is. We never said anything about any money." He turned to the urinal and peed.

"But I didn't think we were going to find anything," I whined. "Besides, it would be compensation for what your sister took."

"I'm not her goddamn keeper."

"But my gun alone . . ."

"Look, do you want to know where my sister is or not?" He buttoned his pants indignantly.

Just then the white man toppled off the seat, banging his head against the washbowl. He slid to the floor, his hat upside down in the basin.

"We been drunk for practically a week." Dougie grinned, disappearing out the door.

I looked down at the pale sleeper's face. His red hair seemed strangely out of place among the white fixtures. I placed the hat over his eyes to shield them from the glare.

Dougie was not in the bar. I ran to the door and looked up and down the street, but he was not in sight. A big yellow Buick was parked at the curb. It was covered with mud, the only clean part the windshield where the wipers had fanned their trails.

Although I knew it would be useless, I searched all the bars and cafés in town, even the hotel and movie house. I paid seventy-five cents to walk up and down the aisle until the usher, a young bald man, told me to either sit down or leave. Bewildered, I sat down and looked at the screen but nothing made sense. I recognized Doris Day. She was drunk and had gotten her toe stuck in a bottle. Then I remembered the Buick. I ran down to Minough's, but the car was gone.

The rain continued to fall. My shoulders slumped under the weight of my soaked jacket and my leg ached. In the gray light of dusk, the sidewalk glistened beneath Minough's neon sign.

## 15

"Nothing to be done about it," the man said. He dabbed his cigar into the bottom of the ashtray. "Happens all the time—hell, you're not unique. Happened to me plenty of times."

We were sitting at the bar of the Pomp Room, which was connected to the Regent's Roost Hotel. The man was from New York. He had shown me his credit cards when I said I didn't believe him.

"Well, you take me—do I look like the sort who would run out on a wife and two beautiful daughters? Hell, by your standards, I was a rich man!"

"You look rich enough to me," I said, and he did. He had on one of those khaki outfits that African hunters wear. I thought of McLeod and Henderson in the *Sports Afield*. His outfit was crisp, with a flowery handkerchief tied around his neck.

"Well, that's another story . . . we're trying to solve your problems."

Problems?

"Of course."

The only problem I had now was trying to stay out of the way of the man I had helped Dougie roll. That was the only problem that was still clear to me. The others had gone away.

"Chance, dumb unadulterated damn luck—I was on my way to the Middle East, had my tickets in my hand . . ."

I drained off my beer and pointed to the empty bottle.

"Barman! Damned if I didn't just turn around, half-way to the plane and everything, tore up my ticket right in front of her . . ."

My jacket was drying on the stool next to me. I had stopped shivering hours ago, just after he bought me my first boilermaker. I had felt a little self-conscious coming in, but the second one took care of that. Now even the fear of a beating, or even getting killed, was subsiding. I lit one of the cigars that lay on the bar.

". . . picked up my fishing gear and drove away!"

"You won't have much luck here," I said.

45

"What? Fish?"

"You won't have much luck here."

"Caught a mess of them yesterday."

"But there are no fish around here."

"Pike—three of them over five pounds. Caught one big northern in Minnesota that ran over thirty."

"That was Minnesota. That wasn't here. You'd be lucky to catch a cold here."

"Caught some nice little rainbows too. Pan size."

"There aren't any rainbows."

He looked at me. He was a big man, soft and healthy, like a baby. He combed his gray hair straight back, so that his red-veined nose seemed too big for his face.

"Tell you what—" He snorted into his hand. "I'll take you out with me tomorrow and if we don't catch any fish, I'll buy you the biggest steak in—where are we?— Malta! You have an outfit?"

"At home—but that's fifty miles away."

"No problem. I've got a spinning rig you can use. Furthermore, I'll use my fly rod and if I don't catch more fish than you, you can have both outfits. Now you can't beat that deal."

I calculated how much both outfits would be worth. "What if neither one of us catches any fish?"

"I'll throw in the biggest steak in Kalamazoo."

"There are no fish in the river," I said confidently. "Not even a sucker."

"Hell . . ." He winked at the bartender, who had been listening, then ordered another boilmaker for me and a double Scotch for himself. "Get one for yourself," he called after the bartender.

Two men in suits opened the door. Then, as though they realized this was the wrong place, they hesitated.

46

After a short conversation, they came in, moving down the bar like cows on slick ice, their eyes not yet adjusted to the dimness of the small blue lights in the ceiling. As they passed me, I smelled the wet wool of their suits. One of them giggled.

The bartender followed them down the other side of the bar as though he were stalking them. He was a skinny man. His red vest and black string tie made him look like a frontier gambler. But he knew all the baseball scores and had been to New York once.

Standing a few feet away from me, a barmaid leaned on her tray. She poked the ice cubes in her Coke with her finger and glared at herself in the mirror. Although I couldn't see a cigarette near her, she was blowing smoke rings.

The two men sat down on the other side of the man who had torn up his airplane ticket.

"What do you think—shall I ask them?"

"About the fish?"

"What else? What else were we talking about? Or would you rather admit you made a mistake?"

I shook my head. "You said you caught a mess of goldeyes?"

"Did I say that? But you're mistaken—there aren't any goldeyes in this river. I've never even heard of goldeyes." He turned to the men in suits. "This man says there are no fish around here."

The two suits looked up. One had a red tie.

"He says there are no fish around here," he repeated.

"Why, that's false," the first suit said. "There are pike in the reservoir south of town. Just the other day I caught a nice bunch."

"In the reservoir south of town," the second suit said.

47

"Ah, you see," said the man who had torn up his airplane ticket.

"But not in the river. It is too muddy and the fish can't see your bait."

"Not likely. It's clear and cold and the fish are firm."

"Yes," said the second suit. "Just the other day my wife and her girl friend fished in the river and they said it was clear and cold."

"I have often remarked on the clarity of the water. It isn't muddy like the reservoir south of town." First suit tasted his drink. He fished out a cherry and nibbled at it. "No matter—no fish there anyway."

"In the reservoir?" I asked.

"Hell no," said the man who had torn up his airplane ticket. "In the creek west of here. The reservoir is full of sunfish."

Second suit, who had finished his drink, ordered another round. He lifted his replenished glass to the mirror and said: "I don't understand these people around here."

"Neither do I," said the man who had torn up his airplane ticket. "Hell—it's uncanny."

I began to feel the effects of the boilermakers. I winked at myself in the mirror and the barmaid, who had returned, glared back.

"I don't understand the people around here—like that man down there." I pointed down the bar to second suit. He was fiddling with a camera.

"I wouldn't know—I'm new here." She blew more smoke rings. There was still no cigarette near her.

"Wait a minute, just a minute here." The man who had torn up his airplane ticket looked past me at the girl. "Don't I know you from someplace?"

48

"How should I know?"

"But I've seen you before, somewhere else. My memory is like a steel trap." He narrowed his eyes. "Bismarck? North Dakota?"

She shook her head.

"Minneapolis?"

She blew a smoke ring at the mirror.

"That's funny. You sure it wasn't Chicago?"

"I've never been there. I might be from the West Coast."

"That's it! Seattle!" His elbow bounced off my ribs. "Ha, you see?"

"Seattle?" I asked.

"I wouldn't be from Seattle for all the rice in China." She counted some coins on her tray. "Now, Portland might be different—they've got roses there."

"My mother raises morning glories," I said.

"Los Angeles?"

"I hate morning glories. I hate anything to do with morning."

"But that's just the name. They bloom in the evening too—even at night I can smell them outside my window. Our cat used to lie in them because it was cool."

"Our cat smothered my baby sister. He lay on her face one night and she couldn't breathe. She would have looked just like me, only she had a birthmark right here." She pressed her finger into the side of her neck. She leaned closer, still without looking at me, and whispered: "That's why he thinks he knows me. He remembers my sister's birthmark."

"But why doesn't he remember you?"

"San Francisco?"

"Oh, he will. Can't you see he's trying right now?"

49

"San Francisco?"

"I used to dance all the time. That's why he doesn't remember me, because I was always dancing and the faster I danced the less he saw of me."

"But he's from New York," I said.

"He used to pay me. That's why I hated it. He used to pay me a dollar to dance for him." She laughed. "It was such fun, twirling around the room, faster and faster until I must have been a blur. That's why he forgets my face."

"San Francisco? Santa Rosa! My wife was from Santa Rosa but she's dead now."

"I could just tell him who I am. Do you think I should?"

"No," I said. "Let him guess."

"I suppose . . . but it might make him mad. That's one thing you learn about men—you don't joke with them unless you mean business." She picked up her tray and walked back to the booths.

The two suits watched her.

"Nice little twitch," said the first suit. His red necktie had worked its way out of his coat.

"Yes," said the second suit. "I wouldn't mind a little bit of that myself."

"Ah, but she would wear you out. You can tell by the hips."

"My wife has hips like that and it's all I can do to stay in bed with her."

"My wife has hips like that," I said, "but she has smaller breasts."

"Small breasts are best," said second suit. "My wife has big breasts and they just get in the way. What you can't get in your mouth is wasted anyway."

50

"My wife has breasts that hang down to her knees and her nipples are too dark."

"Pink nipples are easily the best," I said.

"My wife is dead," said the man who had torn up his airplane ticket.

The bartender brought us a round of drinks on the house and recited some baseball scores. The airplane man continued to name places, but the barmaid wasn't there. Second suit fumbled with his camera. He had the insides out and the film was hanging down over the counter.

My leg had gone numb, as though waterlogged by the boilermakers. At least it didn't ache.

When the barmaid returned, I looked at her breasts. They were not as large as I had thought; her white blouse was a little small, stretched tight across them, straining the button between them.

The airplane man jerked his thumb at me and said: "This man doesn't believe there are goldeyes in the river."

"Of course there are," she said. "I caught seven of them just this morning."

"You can't mean it."

"Positively."

The airplane man glared at her. Suddenly he jerked upright and roared—I thought first suit had stuck a knife in his back—then rushed her, arms extended as if to hug or strangle her. At the last instant, he swerved and hit the door, plunging into the night.

The barmaid smiled at me. "It's still raining."

"You should have danced for him," I said.

"No." She shook her head sadly. "It wouldn't be the same."

## 16

I awoke the next morning with a hangover. I had slept
fitfully, pursued by the ghosts of the night before and
nights past. There were the wanted men with ape faces,
cuffed sleeves and blue hands. They did not look directly
into my eyes but at my mouth, which was dry and hollow of words. They seemed on the verge of performing
an operation. Suddenly a girl loomed before my face,
slit and gutted like a fat rainbow, and begged me to turn
her loose, and I found my own guts spilling from my
monstrous mouth. Teresa hung upside down from a
wanted man's belt, now my own belt, crying out a series
of strange warnings to the man who had torn up his
airplane ticket and who was now rolling in the manure
of the corral, from time to time washing his great pecker
in a tub of water. The gutted rainbow turned into the
barmaid of last night screaming under the hands of the
leering wanted men. Teresa raged at me in several voices,
her tongue clicking against the roof of her mouth. The
men in suits were feeling her, commenting on the texture
of her breasts and the width of her hips. They spread
her legs wider and wider until Amos waddled out, his
feathers wet and shining, one orange leg crocked at the
knee, and suddenly lifted, in a flash of white stunted
wing, up and through a dull sun. The wanted men fell
on the gutted rainbow and second suit clicked pictures
of a woman beside a reservoir in brown light.

I climbed with Teresa's voice still in my head. Although the words were not clear, they were accompa-
nied by another image, that of a boy on horseback racing

down a long hill, yelling and banging his hat against his thigh. Strung out before him, a herd of cattle, some tumbling, some flying, all laughing. The boy was bundled up against a high wind.

I didn't know whether I was asleep or awake during this last scene, but the boy changed quickly into a pale ceiling. The room was stuffy and smelled of liquor. Sun streamed through the white curtains of a tall, narrow window. The curtains were hung about a foot below the top of the window and through this space I could see sky, without depth, as though the window itself were painted a flat blue.

I swung my legs over the edge of the bed, sat up and waited for my head to ache. A quick numbing throb made my eyes water, followed by a wild pounding that seemed to drive my head down between my shoulders. I closed my eyes, opened them, then closed them again —I couldn't make up my mind whether to let the room in on my suffering or keep it to myself. I sat for what seemed like two or three nauseating hours until an over-powering thirst drove me to the sink. I drank a long sucking bellyful of water from the tap, my head pounding fiercely until I straightened up and wiped my mouth. I gripped the sink and waited. Gradually the pounding lessened and I was able to open my eyes again. I stared at my face. It didn't look too bad—a little puffy, pale but lifelike. I soaked one of the towels in cold water and washed up. My pants were knotted down around my ankles. One shoe and one white sock stuck out beneath them. Above them, the vertical scars flanking my left kneecap and the larger bone-white slash running diagonally across the top. Keeping my head up, I reached down and slowly pulled up the pants.

Ah, there was the clean shirt—but then I remembered I had left my paper bag of possessions at Minough's. And I had helped roll the big red-headed cowboy. He was probably out looking for me right now. I wondered if he could recognize me or if he had been too drunk. No, he couldn't, I decided; he was passed out, after all. But somebody at the bar might have described me or given him my name. I couldn't remember if anybody had been in the bar. Of course—the bartender. How could I explain that I had come to Malta only to find a girl who had stolen from me, and that it was only an odd circumstance that led me to steal from him, or at least try? No, he would not understand. The girl, the one item we had in common, would lead to my downfall sure as hell . . .

I cursed Dougie and his sister for bringing me to such a sorry pass, and I cursed the white man for being such a fool and my hotel room for being such a tiny sanctuary on a great earth of stalking white men. I cursed the loss of my possessions, for my teeth were mossy and my shirt lay wrinkled and stained across the sunlit bedspread.

A corner of the bed had been turned down. I must have tried to get into it before passing out. The sheets looked so clean and cool, so white, that I thought about taking off my clothes and slipping down between them. But it was too late, the sun too high.

I wet my hair and combed it with my fingers. Then I slipped my Levi jacket on over my T-shirt—the shirt was awful, I must have vomited—and left the room, walking down the hall first to the toilet, then to the carpeted stairs. The desk clerk didn't look up. A group of old men sat on the orange-vinyl couches in the lobby.

Two of them leaned forward on their canes, while the rest repeated the sagging curves of the furniture. They were watching baseball on the television. I walked quickly by them and out into the sunshine. A woman said excuse me.

## 17

It was Saturday. Children in blue jeans and striped T-shirts ran by me, their small shoes and boots clicking against the sidewalk. Their fathers, some with new haircuts, would be gathered in the bars and cafés to discuss the business they had discussed last Saturday and the Saturday before that, while their wives shopped, careful to avoid the stares of the young men in Levi's and floral cowboy shirts who lounged on the corners or sat on car hoods, talking about girls and cars. The girls touched their hair.

Saturday, and I walked down the hot side of the street to the bar by the railroad station. A woolly-headed man stood beside the cash register picking lint from his black shirt. Except for him the place was deserted.

"What's your pleasure?"

I ordered a Coke and a bag of potato chips, then removed my jacket. The man picked lint from his shirt. A dog wandered in, sniffed my pants cuffs and wandered out.

"It's going to be a hot one, good for business," the man said without looking up. He turned around. "How's my back?"

"Worse than the front," I said.

"I was afraid of that." He looked at me. "You're from up the valley, aren't you?"

"Past Dodson a little ways."

"Reservation?"

"Yep."

"You're Teresa First Raise's boy."

"I'm thirty-two."

"She's a good one, that gal—one of the liveliest little gals I know of."

"She's bigger than you are, bigger than both of us put together."

"Amen—you can say that again." His eyes rolled. "And what is she doing for herself these days?"

"I guess the latest thing she did was marry Lame Bull."

"No!" He slapped his hand on the bar and rolled his eyes again. "Lively little gal . . ."

"They got married a couple of weeks ago. Right here."

"Not by me." He laughed. "Not here."

"No." I laughed. "Down at the courthouse. But I'll bet if they came here that day, you'd sure as hell know it."

He stopped laughing. "Kind of a heavyset guy, bushy hair?"

"Let's see . . ." I noticed that his eyes had gone hard. "No, he's pretty tall, slick hair, kind of skinny."

The bartender scratched his own woolly head. "Nope, nope . . . but I remember that bushy-haired fella. He tried to tune up one of my best customers."

"Oh yes," I said. "He's mean—I know him, slightly—especially on wine."

"I don't mind a guy raising a little hell, but when he

starts tuning up my customers . . . Well, I have to draw the line somewhere, don't I?"

"I don't know him hardly at all, just vaguely."

A train started up over by the railroad station. The sudden jerk on the couplings loosed an explosion that shot through the late morning air, followed by the grinding squeal of steel against steel.

"Say, will you do me a favor?"

"Sure," I said.

"I have to bleed my lizard—if anybody comes in, you just give a holler."

"Sure," I said. "Leave it to me."

Leave it to me. But where was the airplane man—where did he take off to? What about his wife and daughters? Could he have thought the barmaid was his daughter? Deep inside, I felt uneasy about the barmaid, a feeling almost of shame. But why, what had I done? I hadn't intruded on their relationship, that was sure, for there was nothing between them—he was from the east, and she from the west, they couldn't have known each other. Or it had been a joke, they had played a trick on me—but for what purpose, I was nothing to anybody. Or—that's it, I had imagined the whole thing in my drunken state. Neither of them existed, I couldn't even remember—nice twitch—her hips or her breasts —the button of her blouse strained between them. It had been part of my deam—the whole business about the fish, the two suits, her dancing—but why the feeling, the feeling . . .

Then it was before the dream or the first part of the dream—the hotel room, the lamp, me laughing on the bed, her standing above me, me pulling her down, popping the button between her breasts, up again, standing, turning down the bed, pants down around my ankles, her pulling off a shoe, laughing, protesting, reaching for her . . .

I tried to clear my head, to empty it of these images, start again, but all I could see clearly was the moment alone on the bed, the lamplight in my eyes—but it must have happened, she must have come to the room with me.

A customer came in. I didn't look around, but I heard the footsteps and the squeak of the barstool. The bartender had appeared as if by instinct the moment I opened my mouth. As he passed me, he picked a piece of lint from his sleeve. The sun came in the door and crossed my hand. I took a sip of Coke.

The toothbrush, the one I had bought in Dodson! I grabbed my jacket from the stool and patted the pocket. No, I must have dropped it in my sack of possessions that I no longer possessed. But something else . . . I opened the pocket and pulled out a crumpled letter—the letter to Teresa from the priest in Harlem.

Teresa First Raise. Box 85. Dodson, Montana. The handwriting was like a child's, both timid and bold, the letters big, solid, unreal. T-E-R-E-S-A. The name did not belong to the woman who was my mother. It belonged to somebody I didn't know, somebody so far away that the picture on the stamp of a man I didn't recognize seemed familiar.

I wanted to read it, to see what a priest would have to say to a woman who was his friend. I had heard of priests having drinking partners, fishing partners, but never a woman partner. I wanted to read it because his woman partner was my mother. But I didn't want to see my mother's name inside the envelope, in a letter written by a white man who refused to bury Indians in their own plots, who refused to set foot on the reservation. I felt vaguely satisfied as I tore up the letter between my legs and let the pieces fall to the floor.

It was Saturday. I heard the clatter of children running on the sidewalk. The customer, a woman in fringed buckskin, walked to the jukebox. Her mouth, her thin nose glared in the light of the machine as she pondered her selections. The bartender had one leg raised, his foot resting on the beer cooler. He was reading *Popular Science*. I could have reached out and touched his woolly head.

# Part
# Two

## 18

First old Bird tried to bite me; then he tried a kick as I reached under his belly for the cinch. His leg came up like a shot turkey's, throwing him off-balance, and he lurched away from me. He tried a second kick, this time more gingerly, and when his hoof struck the ground, I snaked the cinch up under his belly and tightened down. As soon as he felt the strap taut against his ribs, he puffed his belly up and stood like a bloated cow. He looked satisfied, chewing on the bit. He was very old. I rammed my elbow into his rib cage and the air came out with a whoosh, sending him skittering sideways in surprise. The calf stood tense and interested by the loading chute. Lame Bull cradled his chin on his arms on the top rail of the corral and smiled.

It was a hot morning and I was sweating as I grabbed the saddle horn, turned the stirrup forward and placed my foot in it to swing aboard. As soon as Bird felt my weight settle on his back, he backed up, stumbled and almost went down. Then we took off, crow-hopping around the corral, old Bird hunkering beneath me, jumping straight up and down, suddenly sunfishing, kicking his back legs straight out, and twisting, grunting. We circled the corral four times, each jolt jarring my teeth as I came down hard in the saddle. He started to run, racing stiff-legged at the corral posts, changing directions at the last instant to make another run. Each time we passed Lame Bull, I could see him out of the corner of my eye, head thrown back, roaring at the big white horse and the intent, terrified rider, both hands on the saddle horn, swaying in the wrong direction each time the horse swerved. The calf had started to run, staying just ahead of Bird, bucking and kicking and crapping and bawling for its mother, who was circling on the other side of the corral.

Finally Lame Bull opened the gate, ducking out of the way as calf, horse and rider shot by him out onto the sagebrush flat between the toolshed and slough. I gave Bird his head as we pounded clouds of dust from the Milk River valley. The escaped calf had peeled off and pulled up short, swinging its head from side to side, not sure whether to follow us or return to its mother. We were beyond the big irrigation ditch by the time Bird slowed down and settled into a nervous trot. He panted and rumbled inside, as though a thunderstorm were growing in his belly. We reached the first gate and he was walking, trying to graze the weeds on the side of the road. I got down and opened the gate, leading him through and shutting it. A garter snake slithered off through the long grass, but he didn't see it.

We followed the fence line to the west between a field of alfalfa and another of bluejoint. Through the willows that lined the banks of the irrigation ditch I could see our small white house and the shack in front where Mose and I used to stretch muskrat pelts. The old root cellar where Teresa had seen a puff adder was now a tiny mound off to the side of the granary. A crane flapped above the slough, a gray arrow bound for some distant target.

Bird snorted. He had caught his breath and now walked cautiously with his head high and his dark eyes trained on the horizon in front of us. I slapped a horsefly from his neck but he didn't shy, didn't seem to notice.

"Tired already?" I said. "But you're an old war pony, you're supposed to go all day—at least that's what you'd have us believe."

He flicked his ears as if in irritation but lumbered ahead.

My bad leg had begun to ache from the tenseness with which I had to ride out Bird's storm. I got down and loosened the cinch. He took a walking crap as I led him down the fence line toward the main irrigation ditch. The wooden bridge was rotten. There were holes in the planks and one could see the slow cloudy water filled with bugs and snaky weeds. Bird balked at crossing. I coaxed him with soft words and threats, at last talking him across and down the bank on the other side.

Before us stood a log-and-mud shack set into the ground. The logs were cracked and bleached but the mud was dark, as though it had been freshly applied. There were no windows, only a door dug out of the earth which banked its walls. The weeds and brush stopped a hundred feet away on all sides, leaving only a caked white earth floor that did not give under one's feet. The river flowed through jagged banks some distance away. The old man stood at the edge. As we approached, he lifted his head with the dignity of an old dog sniffing the wind.

"Howdy," I said. The sun flared off the skin of earth between us. "Hello there, Yellow Calf."

He wore no shoes. His suit pants bagged at the knees and were stained on the thighs and crotch by dirt and meals, but his shirt, tan with pearl snaps, seemed clean, even ironed.

"How goes it?" I said.

He seemed confused.

"I'm First Raise's son—I came with him once."

"Ah, of course! You were just a squirt," he said.

"It was during a winter," I said.

"You were just a squirt."

I tied Bird to the pump and pumped a little water into the enamel basin under the spout. "My father called you Yellow Calf . . ." The water was brown. I loosened the bridle and took the bit out of Bird's mouth. It must have tasted strange after so many years. "And now Teresa says you are dead. I guess you died and didn't know it."

"How's that—dead?" He dug his hands into his pockets. "Sometimes I wish . . . but not likely."

"Then you're still called Yellow Calf."

"I'm called many things but that one will do. Some

call me Bat Man because they think I drink the blood of their cattle during the night."

I laughed. "But you should be flattered. That means they are afraid of you."

"I have no need to be flattered. I am old and I live alone. One needs friends to appreciate flattery."

"Then you must be a wise man. You reject friends and flattery."

He made fists in his pants pockets and gestured with his head toward the shack. "I have some coffee."

It was only after he started walking, his feet seeming to move sideways as well as forward, that I realized he was completely blind. It was odd that I hadn't remembered, but maybe he hadn't been blind in those days.

He gripped the doorframe, then stood aside so that I could pass through first. He followed and closed the door, then reopened it. "You'll want some light."

The inside of the shack was clean and spare. It contained a cot, a kitchen table and two chairs. A small wood stove stood against the far wall. Beside the pipe a yellowed calendar hung from the wall. It said December 1936. A white cupboard made up the rest of the furniture in the room. Yellow Calf moved easily, at home with his furnishings. He took two cups, one porcelain, the other tin, from the cupboard and poured from a blackened pot that had been resting on the back of the stove. I coughed to let him know where I was, but he was already handing me a cup.

"Just the thing," I said.

"It's too strong. You're welcome." He eased himself down on the cot and leaned back against the wall.

It was cool, almost damp in the banked shack, and I thought of poor old Bird tied to the pump outside. He might get heatstroke.

"You're a good housekeeper, old man."

"I have many years' practice. It's easier to keep it sparse than to feel the sorrows of possessions."

"Possessions can be sorrowful," I agreed, thinking of my gun and electric razor.

"Only when they are not needed."

"Or when they are needed—when they are needed and a man doesn't have them."

"Take me—I don't have a car," he said.

"But you don't seem to need one. You get along."

"It would be easier with a car. Surely you have one."

"No."

"If you had a car you could take me to town."

I nodded.

"It would make life easier," he went on. "One wouldn't have to depend on others."

I wondered how the old man would drive a car. Perhaps he had radar and would drive only at night.

"You need a good pair of shoes to drive a car," I said.

"I have thought of that too." He tucked his feet under the cot as though they were embarrassed.

"There are probably laws against driving barefoot, anyway."

He sighed. "Yes, I suppose there are."

"You don't have to worry—not out here."

"I wouldn't say that."

"How so?"

"Irrigation man comes every so often to regulate the head gate—he keep his eye on me. I can hear him every so often down by that head gate."

I laughed. "You're too nervous, grandfather—besides, what have you got to hide, what have you done to be ashamed of?"

"Wouldn't you like to know . . ." His mouth dropped and his shoulders bobbed up and down.

"Come on, tell me. What have you got in those pants?"

"Wouldn't you like to know . . ." With that, his mouth dropped open another inch but no sound came out.

"I'll bet you have a woman around here. I know how you old buzzards operate."

His shoulders continued to shake, then he started coughing. He coughed and shook, holding his cup away from the cot, until the spasm of mirth or whatever it was had passed.

He stood and walked to the stove. When he reached for my cup, his hand struck my wrist. His fingers were slick, papery, like the belly of a rattlesnake. He poured to within half an inch of the cup's lip, to the tip of the finger he had placed inside.

"How is it you say you are only half dead, Yellow Calf, yet you move like a ghost. How can I be sure you aren't all the way dead and are only playing games?"

"Could I be a ghost and suck the blood of cattle at the same time?" He settled back on the cot, his lips thinned into what could have been a smile.

"No, I suppose not. But I can't help but feel there's something wrong with you. No man should live alone."

"Who's alone? The deer come—in the evenings—they come to feed on the other side of the ditch. I can hear them. When they whistle, I whistle back."

"And do they understand you?" I said this mockingly. His eyes were hidden in the darkness.

"Mostly—I can understand most of them."

"What do they talk about?"

"It's difficult . . . About ordinary things, but some of them are hard to understand."

"But do they talk about the weather?"

"No, no, not that. They leave that to men." He sucked on his lips. "No, they seem to talk mostly about . . ."—he searched the room with a peculiar alertness—"well, about the days gone by. They talk a lot about that. They are not happy."

"Not happy? But surely to a deer one year is as good as the next. How do you mean?"

"Things change—things have changed. They are not happy."

"Ah, a matter of seasons! When their bellies are full, they remember when the feed was not so good—and when they are cold, they remember . . ."

"No!" The sharpness of his own voice startled him. "I mean, it goes deeper than that. They are not happy with the way things are. They know what a bad time it is. They can tell by the moon when the world is cockeyed."

"But that's impossible."

"They understand the signs. This earth is cockeyed."

A breeze came up, rustling the leaves of the tall cottonwoods by the ditch. It was getting on in the afternoon.

I felt that I should let the subject die, but I was curious about Yellow Calf's mind.

"Other animals—do you understand them?"

"Some, some more than others."

"Hmmm," I said.

"This earth is cockeyed."

"Hmmm . . ."

"Of course men are the last to know."

"And you?"

"Even with their machines."

"Hmmm . . ."

"I have my inclinations."

"The moon?"

"Among other things—sometimes it seems that one has to lean into the wind to stand straight."

"You're doing plenty of leaning right now, I would say," I said.

"You don't believe the deer." He was neither challenging nor hurt. It was a statement.

"I wouldn't say that."

"You do not believe me."

"It's not a question of belief. Don't you see? If I believe you, then the world is cockeyed."

"But you have no choice."

"You could be wrong—you could believe and still be wrong. The deer could be wrong."

"You do not want to believe them."

"I can't."

"It's no matter."

"I'm sorry."

"No need—we can't change anything. Even the deer can't change anything. They only see the signs."

A pheasant sounded to the east but the old man either did not pay attention or thought it a usual message. He leaned forward into the shadows of the shack, holding his cup with both hands, looking directly at me and through me. I shifted from one buttock to the other, then set my cup on the table.

"It's not very good," he said.

"No—that's not true. It's just that I have to leave; we're weaning a calf . . ."

"I'm old."

"Yes."

"You must say hello to Teresa for me. Tell her that I am living to the best of my ability."

"I'll tell her to come see for herself," I said.

"Say hello to First Raise."

"Yes, yes . . . he will be pleased." Didn't he know that First Raise had been dead for ten years?

We walked out into the glare of the afternoon sun.

Bird tried to kick me as I swung my leg over his back. "Next time I'll bring some wine," I said.

"It is not necessary," he said.

"For a treat."

I started to wave from the top of the bridge. Yellow Calf was facing off toward the river, listening to two magpies argue.

# 19

Lame Bull jerked the pickup up the incline and pointed it west toward Harlem. He double-clutched the gears into high, then took a long gurgling pull from the bottle of beer he had between his thighs. An Eddy's Bread truck roared past us from behind. Lame Bull waved and honked. Teresa sat between us, the sack of beer at her feet.

"You're going to kill us yet," she said.

He laughed. "You just wait till we hit that straight-away down by White Bear. By God, I'll show you some driving."

She turned to me. "And what kind of nonsense are you going to pull this time? First you lose your best shirt, then you almost kill poor Bird—what's next on your agenda?"

"Leave the boy alone," Lame Bull said. "I was plenty wild myself when I was his age."

"I'm thirty-two," I said. Sometimes I had to tell myself.

"And you never recovered—now you try to kill us."

"I think you're due for a long walk, old woman."

"You seem to forget that I own this car."

Lame Bull took his foot off the gas pedal. "You want to drive?" Then just as quickly he pressed the pedal to the floor. "All right then . . ." He leaned forward and winked at me. "Boy, you're going to catch her this time, I feel it in my bone—I mean bones—catchum, holdum, shrinkum—you got to treat these women rough once in a while or else they forget." He squeezed the inside of Teresa's thigh.

The water behind the dam at White Bear was down. It was a good time to catch turtles.

"You and your brother used to ride Bird down here for a swim—do you remember that? She rested her hand on Lame Bull's.

"I was just thinking about that," I said.

"Do you remember the day you boys got caught in that lightning storm? Your cousin Charley was with you. You all three rode down here on old Bird."

"He wasn't old then. He was barely three years old." A three-year-old the year Mose got killed.

"Nevertheless you all three rode him."

"We took shelter under those trees," I said, pointing

71

to a stand of cottonwoods. "Mose built a lean-to out of the old branches. We stuck it out, but Bird ran home —he didn't understand the lightning."

"The only thing he understands is a good swift kick in the slats," Lame Bull said.

We had watched Bird take off, reins flying straight back, his shoulders bunched and legs a white streak in the downpour. Each time a slice of lightning crackled down, he jumped straight into the air. We watched him out of sight, then Mose gathered branches and willows for the lean-to. He was very deliberate, cutting and notching two poles and a crosspiece, until he was ready to lay the branches across. Charley and I stood soaked under one of the trees. The lightning crashed down around us, but Mose worked until the shelter was completed. He scooted under and grinned at us.

Then there was the fire—he borrowed Charley's matches, struck one and placed the flame in a small hole in a pile of twigs and leaves. "We should have caught a turtle," he said. "If we had a turtle we could cook him and make soup in his own shell." The fire smoked a lot but did little to keep us warm. Mose was satisfied. He kept poking the fire and coughing from the smoke. And the cigarette—we helped Charley smoke one of his Bull Durham cigarettes.

And the magic—as suddenly as it had started, the storm ended, scattering clouds in four directions. The sun burned away the tail ends and danced on the waters of White Bear as we began the long walk home. The roads were dusty again by the time we reached the ranch, and Bird whinnied a welcome from the shadows of the horse shed.

Mose was fourteen; I was twelve.

"You boys had such a time." Teresa laughed.

It was noon when we reached Harlem and dropped her off at the priest's house. He would find out that she hadn't gotten his letter which I had torn up down in Malta. He probably didn't even know Teresa had married Lame Bull. And Lame Bull didn't know anything.

He dropped me by Buttrey's store and drove over to the John Deere place for more baling twine. A few Indians leaned against the buildings in the shade, some with hard hats, ready to go fight fire when the man from the agency came to collect them, others with stetsons and big-buckled belts, ready to help the fire fighters spend their money when they returned. Edgar Bullshoe fell in beside me as I passed Beany's Tavern.

"Hey, cousin, you got a smoke?"

"I gave it up. Ask your cousin Musty there."

Musty walked over and asked for a quarter.

Larue Henderson was checking the oil in a new Chevy. I kicked the bumper. He glanced up at me. As if I had caused him to lose his place, he frowned and pushed the dipstick back into the block. He pulled it out again, held it up to the light, made another face. The oil dripped on the fender. He was satisfied. He closed the car hood.

"Now, what can I do for you?" he said.

I couldn't see his eyes—nobody could see his eyes because he wore black glasses, like a blind man. I don't think anybody had ever seen his eyes, not even his wife. There were times, when I was drunk enough, and he was drunk enough, I could just see something glistening behind the glasses. Lame Bull told me once how he had gotten into a fight with Larue Henderson down at Beany's one night and had knocked those glasses off, and how Larue Henderson just quit and held his hands over his eyes while Lame Bull knocked his teeth out. When Lame Bull had satisfied himself, he walked over to the drugstore and bought Larue Henderson a new pair. It may have been true. Larue Henderson had very few teeth.

He wiped some of the fresher bugs off the windshield of the Chevy, then walked into the station, where the owner of the car was waiting. I followed him.

"Oil's okay, but you better watch that fan belt. I seen healthier looking fan belts in my life."

He charged the man an extra dollar for that advice.

The man wore one of those see-through shirts that look like they're made out of wax paper. He had soft breasts.

"You won't catch any fish around here," I said.

After the man left, Larue Henderson put the extra dollar in his pocket. "Do you know that guy?"

"Maybe," I said. "He looks kind of familiar."

"What brings you to town? I thought you and Lame Bull would be sitting around counting your old lady's money."

"Naw—we're not so rich." But I felt a little proud. To be thought a rich man isn't so bad. "Hell, I'm just looking for somebody."

He was neither impressed nor curious. He opened the display case and grabbed a salted nut roll.

"You want to go get a beer?" I said.

"What the hell's the matter with you guys? Can't you see I'm busy?" He peeled the wrapper off the salted nut roll. "Christ, it's getting tougher all the time to make a living in this damn town."

"I'm buying," I said.

"Jesus Christ," he said, shaking his head. "Okay, okay —just one, just the one you're buying."

He rang the cash register and took out a ten-dollar bill.

"Just a minute." He walked back to the door to the grease pit. "Hey you! You want to watch this garage, understand? And I mean watch it. I don't want you jerking off in the toilet."

A whimper came from the other room.

"Who's that?" I said as we walked across the street.

"Oh, that goddamn kid. He's just reached that stage where all he thinks about is jerking off. Christ, I've found it on the mirror in the bathroom, those tires— even the goddamn souvenirs in the showcase."

We were in the shadow of the bank building.

"Look at those petty bastards, up there counting their money."

I looked up at the plate-glass window, but the venetian blinds were closed.

"I can't fire him. His old lady'd have my ass."

"You own the place, don't you?"

"You kidding—those bastards up there own it." He jerked his thumb at the window. "Christ, they don't even know how to change a tire."

"They own just about everything," I said.

"His old lady'd cut my nuts off."

"How are you and her getting along?"

"Christ, are you kidding?"

Lame Bull was sitting in Beany's. Beany himself was tending bar. He was very old and very white. Also very rich. Lame Bull was telling him about the hardships of being an owner. Beany nodded all the while, his fingers caressing the change on the bar. "It ain't easy," he was saying, "oh, it definitely ain't easy."

Lame Bull insisted on paying for our beers, his arm around me, telling Beany how he was trying to be a good father.

"Oh, it ain't easy . . . being a father." Beany scratched his white head and continued to fondle the change.

"Shit." Larue Henderson lit up one of his Salems.

"See, see," Lame Bull said quickly. "There you go."

"Shit," Larue Henderson said.

"See what I mean?" said Lame Bull.

"Oh, it definitely ain't easy," said Beany.

"Shit," said Larue Henderson for the third time.

"You got a foul mouth and you smoke like a woman —you know that, Larue?"

"Shit," said a woman down the bar.

"Hey, old nightmare, you want a good swift kick in the slats? I got a boot here that'll tickle your tonsils any time you want." Lame Bull squeezed my neck for emphasis.

"What I want you sure as hell ain't got, you old fart."

Lame Bull laughed and squeezed my neck again. "You want to go in the back room and take an estimate?"

"Boy, you old guys . . ." She drained her glass. "Buy me a drink."

Lame Bull bought her a drink.

Larue Henderson hunkered over the bar. I could see the woman beyond the plane of his shoulders. She was around forty. Her lips were dark red and she wore dark makeup around her eyes. Her black hair fell in curls around her shoulders. She was digging for something in her purse.

"How come your boy don't come down and talk to me?" She didn't even look up.

"He's studying to be a priest," Lame Bull said, holding me down by the neck so I couldn't get up.

"Tell him I got something here that'll make him forget them ideas in a goddamn hurry."

Larue Henderson's eyebrows lifted above the rims of his dark glasses. "You mean in that purse?" he said.

"If you can't figure that out, dark eyes, you better go back to your garage and have that boy explain a few things to you." She got out her lipstick.

"Shit."

"Do you know her?" I said.

"If it ain't those goddamn bankers, it's some smartass woman."

"She's on the fight."

"I've seen her around—she's from Havre, big-city woman—shit."

"I wonder if she has a car?"

Musty came up to us and asked for a quarter. He was wearing a red-plastic hunter's cap. Larue Henderson gave him a handful of change and he went away.

"Goddamn Indians . . . How do you think she knows about that garage? She has a car, all right, if you can call one of them damn Volkswagens a car."

"Listen, do you remember when I told you I was looking for somebody?"

"I don't remember."

"Maybe I didn't tell you."

"So what?"

"Well, she's in Havre."

"No kidding—in Havre, of all places."

"Don't you get it?"

"Get what?" He sighed.

"Put two and two together."

"Four."

I laughed.

"Jesus Christ, I must be going insane." He stood and accidentally knocked his stool over.

"Hey, where you going, dark eyes . . . you haven't bought me a drink yet!" The woman giggled.

Larue Henderson walked out the door without turning around.

"He's a real world-beater, ain't he?" the woman said.

"He's troubled by high finances," I said.

"Aren't they all . . ."

I picked up my beer and walked down the bar. When Lame Bull didn't say anything, I looked back. He wasn't there.

"What do you think you're up to?"

"A friendly chat."

"Well, aren't you the one." She held up her empty glass and waggled it.

"Hey, Beany!"

He brought her a shot of whiskey and a glass of water. "A little snake oil for the little lady," he said.

She swore.

"And another beer for me, if you please." I pushed a dollar bill across the counter.

"And now what do you want?" she said, sipping the water.

"You mean right now?"

"Oh brother, you young guys are something else . . ."

She smoked Pall Malls. Several butts were lined neatly in the ashtray, each with the red mark of her lipstick. She shook one out of her pack and put it to her mouth. She wore a diamond ring on her wedding finger. It was very thin underneath, as though it had been worn by somebody every day of several lifetimes. The initials "JR" were tattooed on the flap of skin between her thumb and index finger. The letters were blurred.

"Who's JR?"

"Well, if that doesn't—Jesus!" She threw a book of matches on the bar. "Whew . . . give me a light."

"Where do you come from?" I struck a match and put it to her cigarette.

"Just where I'm going back to as soon as I finish this drink." She sipped her water. "I never met anybody so interested in other people's affairs."

"I'm just trying to be pleasant. Who's JR?"

"He might be my husband—he just might be the man who keeps me busy at night. How about that?"

"I don't know . . . is he?" It was true that I was interested in her affairs.

"That's for me to know and you to find out." She blew a puff of smoke at the ceiling.

"I was just curious—I just thought maybe you'd like to talk about him."

"Well, I wouldn't. That was a long time ago, believe me." She stroked her hair back away from her forehead and continued to smoke.

I leaned back to get a better look at her. I could see only the undersides of her breasts because of her arm, but they must have been large, for they extended far back to a flat belly. Her dress was tight and shiny across her thighs, the dark green reminding me of a mermaid I had seen once.

"I saw that."

"What?" I coughed into my fist.

79

She looked sad or disappointed, pretty in her pose. "I didn't do anything," I said.

"I won't go into it," she said sadly. She crossed her legs away from me and swung her foot in tight loops.

"I'm sorry—where did you say you were from?"

"Havre."

"Havre!"

"Havre," she repeated sadly.

"But that's where I'm going!"

She lifted the glass of whiskey off the bar and looked into it.

"I have to report for work—foreman on the railroad —tomorrow morning . . ."

She put the glass to her lips and held it there. "Foreman, my foot—look at yourself." But she didn't look.

"First thing in the morning, me and my crew . . ."

"Trying to tell me he's a foreman." She tilted the glass and sipped. The whiskey disappeared in six swallows.

"Well, it isn't definite."

"How about another one?"

I signaled to Beany.

"Have you ever ridden on the Empire Builder?" she said.

"The Western Star a couple of times."

"I rode the Empire Builder to Minneapolis once— looking for work." She ran her finger around the rim of the glass.

"It doesn't stop here."

" 'Oh sure,' they said, 'there's plenty of jobs in Minneapolis . . .' " She seemed suddenly bitter, as though the last whiskey had pushed her over a personal edge. "If ninety words a minute isn't good enough for them, then just to hell with them!"

"Is that what you are—a secretary?"

"Not anymore, buster. That was a long time ago, believe me."

"Ah, well, that's how it is."

"You want to know something else?" She looked directly into my face. "Okay, if you must know, I never worked day one as a secretary. Trained for two years at Haskell, learning how to squiggle while some big-nuts shot his mouth off, and never even worked the first day!" There were tears in her eyes. She was drunker than I thought. "It's a lousy world can do that to a girl!"

"It's not great." I was getting depressed myself.

"Look at you, bitching . . ." She turned back to the glass before her. "At least you're going to work in the morning."

"It's not exactly definite." I felt guilty for having lied to her.

"But at least it's something."

"Well, sort of . . ."

"So you want a ride with me; is that what you're getting at?"

Beany brought another shot of whiskey and a beer. He refilled her water glass.

"Well, okay," she said. "If that's what you want, it can be arranged."

So it was settled.

"How can you stand to drink that shit?" she said, pointing at my beer. Her voice shook.

## 20

I couldn't figure out how I ended up on the couch with a rubber-back rug over me. The rubber was cold against my shoulders and the edge bristled under my chin.

Outside the window, a meadowlark announced the first streaks of the morning sun.

I sat up and threw the rug on the floor. The coffee table was pushed back three or four feet. A glass of diluted whiskey filled with red-tipped cigarette butts balanced on the edge. I set it on the floor. I was in the back part of a room built like a boxcar. An oil stove squatted in a corner opposite me, next to it another couch exactly like mine but with a tangle of sheets and blankets. A pillow lay on the floor. There was a bookcase at the head of the couch but no books—just a few knickknacks, a football and what looked to be a plastic recordplayer. The front part of the room was the kitchen, with a whole assortment of cupboards, dirty dishes and greasy wallpaper. A door opened out beside a yellowed refrigerator—it led to the sun-streaked stucco wall of another house. On the other side of the refrigerator, up against the wall, a kitchen table—and a boy, maybe five or six, quietly eating a bowl of cereal.

I stood and slipped into my shirt, buttoning it quickly, tucking it into my pants, conscious of the boy; but from the sound of the spoon in the bowl he was too busy eating to pay much attention.

The door behind me contrasted with the shabby room—-it was new, dark-stained plywood with a glass knob. I turned the knob and peeked into a bedroom: the woman, Malvina (she wouldn't tell me her last

name), lay asleep in a large bed. I stepped inside and
closed the door behind me. There wasn't much in the
way of furniture—a dresser, a wooden chair, a small
table beside the bed—but the room was coated with
lace and ruffles, the window hidden behind a ruffled
curtain, even the bedspread was ruffled. It was like
being inside a cocoon. Perfume lay heavy on the air,
beneath it the faint smell of whiskey.

The dresser was covered with bottles of perfume
and cologne, talcs and powder puffs, all delicately
colored, all nestled deep in ruffles. Bubble-bath globes
lay scattered among the bottles. I picked one up and
felt its smoothness. It was light blue, almost trans-
parent. I remembered the cold spring day Mose and I
had found the bubble-bath globes in Teresa's bedroom.
My father must have given them to her as a present,
perhaps for Christmas or her birthday. They were
packed in a clear plastic box with a ribbon around it.
Not one had been removed. Now I tried to imagine
Teresa in the metal tub on the bedroom floor up to her
neck in bubbles. First Raise was not a practical man.

I sat down on the edge of Malvina's bed. Beside it
the table glittered solemnly with gold picture frames.
I tilted one toward the window. There was Malvina,
younger, prettier, smiling beside a shiny '53 Buick;
another picture showed her in the doorway of a dark
cabin, another before a cannon in some public square—
all the pictures were of Malvina alone in various places,
in various dress, always smiling, although I didn't think
she smiled much. I couldn't remember her smiling at
all last night. I wondered who held the camera—was it
JR?—or did she have one that took pictures by itself?

She lay on her side with her back to me. I lifted the

83

sheet away from her body. Her brown shoulder glowed in the shuttered light. I leaned toward her. Her breasts were very large, silky, tipped with enormous brown nipples. My head grew light from the heavy perfume and a sudden rush of hunger for her. I leaned further and stroked the side of her breast. I eased my hand under it and weighed it, rolling the nipple between my fingertips. I started to reach for the dark hair between her thighs—

"Beat it."

My hand froze.

"Beat it."

My groin froze.

"Beat it."

I dropped the sheet over her and sat for a moment, trying to decide how I should attack her, but the thought of the boy eating cereal in the next room took over and I felt the quick desire dying in my crotch.

I went into the bathroom and peed. Then I washed my face with a bar of soap that looked like a cluster of tiny grapes. As I walked through the bedroom I glanced at the bed—she had rolled over on her back, her breasts spread like puddings beneath the sheet. I shut the door gently.

"What do you say, sport?" I said as I walked by the table.

"My name's not sport," he hissed after me.

## 21

Three of us stood separately under the green awning of the Coast-to-Coast store on Highway 2. The other two looked as if they were waiting for the stores to open. I was waiting for Gable's and The Silver Dollar to open. According to the clock on the bank down the street, we all had twenty minutes to go.

The air was fresh at that hour of morning. The traffic was light, almost nonexistent, although Highway 2 ran east and west through the heart of Havre. The trucks which would be grinding through later had not yet started. Another man joined us, scratching his arm as he studied the brand-new bicycles in the window.

"That three-speed costs eighty-nine dollars," he said.

I walked across the street and entered the Dutch Shoppe restaurant, where I ordered a glass of milk and a piece of cherry pie à la mode. The waitress's uniform rustled crisply as she walked down to the milk cooler. Damn that Malvina.

I had just forked in the first piece of pie when a man suddenly plopped down on the stool next to me. He came so quickly, so quietly, I thought he had dropped out of the ceiling.

"Don't look around," he said. "Remember me?"

The cherries were sour and I tried to keep my mouth shut as I shook my head.

"You don't remember me?" He sounded disappointed.

I swallowed the whole lump. "How can I tell if I can't look around?"

"Oh, I didn't mean that—of course you can look at me." He leaned forward. "I mean, hell!"

I looked at him.

"Now do you remember?" he said. "Just don't look all the way around."

I looked all the way around. The café was empty. I

looked back. He was the man from Malta, the man who had torn up his airplane ticket.

"Hey," I said. I was happy to see a familiar face.

"Ha—ha—you do remember."

"Hey."

"Long time, no see," he said.

"I didn't expect to see you again. You were just a tourist."

"I wouldn't go so far as to say that; I mean, I'm not your average tourist."

"No . . . I didn't mean to offend you. You're quite the wanderer," I said. "How come you don't want me to look around?"

He dropped his elbows on the counter and rubbed his eyes. The words came from the side of his mouth: "I wish you hadn't asked me that. I'd hate to see you get mixed up in this mess."

The waitress tapped her pencil on the counter.

He opened his eyes and with a great air of dignity ordered a cream puff and a cup of coffee.

"In what?" My voice must have risen, for he looked around quickly.

"No, really, forget it. I'd never forgive myself."

"But what are friends for? It's not as if we weren't friends."

"Pass the sugar." He sprinkled a few grains into his coffee.

"I mean it—what are friends for?"

"Pass the cream."

"It's curdled."

"Oh, God—well, listen here a minute." He squinted into my eyes. "Are you sure you want to help?"

I nodded.

"Do you understand what's going on?"

I shook my head.

"Okay, okay, let me fill you in." He stopped short when an old man in a straw hat and green gabardines walked in.

"We've got to get out of here," he whispered.

"What . . . that old man?"

"Precisely. You catch on quickly." As an afterthought, he added: "I like that."

"You never know . . ." I said.

"Where can we go?"

"How about the Legion Club? It should be open by now."

"That's an excellent idea," he whispered. "What say we meet over there? No, don't follow immediately, wait a minute."

He stood and fished a silver dollar out of his safari pants. "Well," he said loudly, "I'd better get cracking!"

"No telling . . ."

"Indeed! For you, honey," he called to the waitress, throwing the dollar on the counter.

"Good luck," I said.

"You're quite kind," he said, tugging his pants up. "I just might do a little fishing."

I looked up at him. "But there are no fish in the river."

He grimaced. Then winked. Then motioned toward the old man. "See you around."

I finished my pie and coffee, then stood up to leave. The old man was rolling a cigarette. He was shaky and the tobacco kept spilling out the ends.

"He's not much of a fisherman," I said. "He deludes himself."

"Heh, heh," said the old man. He licked the paper. A bowl of oatmeal sat on the counter in front of him.

"You're an old-timer. Have you ever known this river to have fish in it?"

"Heh, heh." He held the cigarette up to admire it. Considering his shakiness, he hadn't done a bad job. It was just a little bulgy in the middle. "Heh, heh," he said again. A great crash, as though somebody had dropped a stack of dishes, came from the kitchen. Somebody swore. The old man placed the cigarette between his lips, struck a farmer's match on his fly, inhaled deeply, then plunged facedown into the oatmeal.

It was plain that he was dead. I tapped him on the shoulder just to make sure, but he was dead all right.

## 22

Again I stood under the awning of the Coast-to-Coast store in order to collect my thoughts. Gable's and The Silver Dollar would be open by now, but the girl wouldn't be there, not this early. I felt a peculiar sense of relief. The girl undoubtedly had gotten rid of my gun and electric razor, so what would the confrontation be about? I didn't want her back—I was damned relieved when she left, so why would I want to find her? —but I knew I would search her out again and find her, that afternoon or evening, but not yet. It was too early, and there was the airplane man and whatever mess he was in . . .

"This your car?" A meter maid was writing out a ticket in front of me.

"I wish." I stepped out from under the awning and started down the street, past the movie house, the florist's shop, the liquor store . . .

"I thought you'd never get here," said the airplane man as I entered the Legion Club.

"I almost didn't. I almost got hit by a car," I said.

"No matter—good that you're here." He was talking again in that confidential tone.

"You remember that old man in the café?"

"The eavesdropper."

"Well, he's dead."

He gave me a puzzled look. Then as though he remembered something else, he reached into his pocket and pulled out a handkerchief. He wiped the sweat from his forehead, then blew his nose, a quick snort. "I like the way you think under pressure. I think we're going to get along okay."

"Deader'n a doornail."

"It's just as well . . . dead, you say?"

"Deader'n a doornail. He's just sitting there one minute rolling a cigarette and next thing I know he's a goner."

"It's just as well . . . dead!" He shook his head.

"He won't be eavesdropping anymore."

"I suppose . . . hell, I just can't believe it."

I had expected him to be pleased with this piece of information, but now he was shaking his head and muttering. He wiped his upper lip with the rag. Then blew his nose again.

"At least he won't be trailing you anymore."

"Oh, he wasn't—that was the first time I saw him."

"What?"

"I never saw him before this morning in my life."

"But I thought you said—"

"No, no—as a matter of fact, someone else is tracking me, since you bring it up."

"Well, you won't have to worry about him anyway." I felt like a fool.

The airplane man busied himself with a punchboard. On the top of the board a girl with golden hair lifted her skirt exposing golden thighs. A red heart was stitched on the crotch of her panties. He punched a dozen numbers, unfolding them carefully, then peeking at them with his head tilted. None of the numbers matched the ones on the top of the board. He swept them off the counter and punched a dozen more.

"You aren't very lucky," I said.

"Probably just as well." He punched a dozen more.

"Who is trailing you, then?" I said.

He peeked at another number, then glanced at me. "Well, I'll be damned."

"What?"

"I won. Hey, I won," he yelled down to the bartender.

The bartender, a man in his sixties with a red turkey neck, strolled over, bar rag in hand. "What can I do for you, ace?"

"I won something. See, this number matches the second one in the third column. I won a prize or something."

The bartender pulled a pair of reading glasses from his shirt pocket. He put them on and held the piece of paper up to the light. Then he walked down to the window and looked again. "Is this number on that board?" he called.

"Here." The airplane man held the board up, pointing at a number.

The bartender brought a box of chocolate-covered cherries. "I'm just the swamper here. I'm not really a bartender—hell, you couldn't pay me enough." He looked at us shrewdly. "I just keep the joint clean."

"You do a pretty good job," I said.

"Old Walt, he lets me sleep in the back," he explained. "Now then, how many chances did you take?"

"About thirty, I guess," said the airplane man.

"At a nickel a throw, that adds up to . . ." He closed his eyes. "How much?"

The airplane man rolled his eyes. I shook my head. The swamper got a pad and pencil. He licked his thumb. "Let's see now, thirty times five equals . . ." On the paper he was dividing five into thirty. "Let's just round it off—say, five dollars?"

"That's impossible," I said. "Thirty nickels doesn't add up to five dollars."

The swamper ran the pencil through his hair, scratching his scalp with the point. "I'm just the swamper," he pouted. And he began to draw a column of fives, which at first leaned too far to the left, then to the right. He pushed the pad at me. "How are you at arithmetic, ace?"

A fly lit on my forehead.

"Regular bartender's got woman troubles—if you catch my meaning," the swamper explained.

I began to add up the fives. It wasn't easy because of the curve of the column. Finally, I pushed the pad back to the swamper. He held it up to the light, then walked down to the window. "You owe me one dollar and ninety-five centavos," he said. He was smiling now that the problem had been solved.

The airplane man took two dollars from his wallet

and tossed them on the bar. "Here—and I'll take one more chance for that extra nickel."

The swamper leaned over the money. "Wait a minute —that's not right."

"It'll make things easier. Don't you see, the two bucks will square us."

"Nope, nope—it's going to throw my arithmetic way off. I'm the one who has to ring up this cash register, not you." He rang up the dollar ninety-five and brought the nickel back. "Now, you want another chance, is that it?"

The airplane man seemed dazed.

"Okeydoke, punch away, ace."

He won again. After the ritual by the window, the swamper brought another box of chocolate-covered cherries. "Say, you're one of them lucky ones—me, I'd head for Reno if I had that kind of luck." He turned to me: "What are you drinking, ace?"

I ordered a mug of beer which I didn't want, then walked back to the toilet. *What are you looking up here for? The joke's in your hand.* I buttoned my pants and looked at my face in the mirror. I needed a shave. If I had my electric razor I would be able to shave. But there was no outlet.

A large purple teddy bear was occupying my stool. The floor was littered with punchboard chances. The airplane man was working on a new board, this one with a picture of a señorita raising her flamenco dress. I sat beside the teddy bear, stroking its fuzzy head. It had a white belly and face. Two black-button eyes stared solemnly at the mug of beer and a red felt tongue flopped foolishly from between its lips.

# 23

"Canada!"

"Jesus, not so loud." He leaned across the teddy bear.

"What's that, ace?"

"Nothing, nothing," he called.

"But why Canada—what's up there?"

"It's what isn't up there that concerns me." He put his arm around the teddy bear. "The F.B.I."

"Now just a minute—are you trying to say the F.B.I. is looking for you? Is that the mess you're in?"

"The Federal Bureau of Investigation, correct."

"But what did you do?"

"Took a little something that wasn't exactly mine—absconded, you might say."

"Money?"

"I'm not at liberty to say at the moment. I plead the fifth." He looked smug.

"So now you're on the lam. Shouldn't you be in hiding?"

"I am. I'm hiding in Montana; what better place to hide? Except Canada, of course—and that's where you come in." He ordered another drink, a gin and tonic. "No cherry this time, huh?"

"Right you are, ace."

"Then that business about tearing up your airplane ticket and leaving your wife was all a lie?"

"Not at all! In fact, it was my wife who put the federal men on me." He laughed. "She was burned!"

I pondered this. It seemed a little coldhearted for a wife to squeal on her husband, but then he *had* run out on her.

"I don't have a car," I said.

"No problem. For that matter we can go get one right now, if you like."

"And you just want me to drive you across the border and that's all?"

"That's it."

"Those border guards get pretty cranky sometimes."

"I've thought of that, but, see—and this is the beauty of it—we tell them that you're driving me up to Calgary to catch a plane. That way you can come back alone, no questions asked." He slapped the teddy bear on the shoulder.

"How will I come back?"

"Alone—that's the beauty of it."

"No, I mean how will I get back? I can't just walk back."

"You think I'd let you walk back? What do you take me for—Mussolini? No, here's how it'll be, see. You drop me in Calgary and the car is yours. You come whistling back in style."

"Where you going to catch the plane to?"

"That's my business—this is strictly business. Once we get past the border, you'll receive five hundred plus the car. Now tell me that's not worth your while."

"I can't figure out why you picked me—maybe I should tell you, those guards like to harass Indians. They can never figure out why an Indian should want to go to Canada."

"Man, you don't know anything about intrigue!" He

slapped the teddy bear on the head. "Now listen: there are two of us in the car, right? One of us gets harassed; you said it, right? In fact the harassed one is going to keep those guards so busy harassing him that they aren't going to pay any attention to the other one. I'm going to drive across, see—I'll just say I picked you up. Now who do you suppose is going to question me?"

I looked out the door. There was an ambulance double-parked across the street. The driver was reading a newspaper. He seemed to be laughing at something he was reading.

"When do you want to do this?" I asked.

"Tonight . . . when the moon is full." He rested his chin on the teddy bear and glared at me. His blue eyes seemed lazy and wild at the same time, as though the swamper had slipped him a knockout drop and he hadn't quite reacted.

## 24

I felt like a fool carrying the purple teddy bear through the streets of Havre. The airplane man walked behind me and off to the side. He had five boxes of chocolate-covered cherries under his arm.

"You ought to see yourself," he said. "A grown man, too . . ."

"Look," I said, "couldn't we just get rid of this damn thing? It's not like we're obliged to take it with us."

"It's for my daughter—I'm going to wrap it up and send it to her. Trouble with you is you don't appreciate good old-fashioned sentiment." But he kept walking off to the side. "That's the trouble with you young buckeroos."

"Well, whatever it is, I'm beginning to feel like an idiot."

"See?"

"Besides, don't you think we might be attracting a little too much attention? You're supposed to be an outlaw."

Two girls approached us. One was swinging her purse against the other's behind in rhythm to their step. I hid behind the teddy-bear head. They giggled. The airplane man offered them each a box of chocolate-covered cherries. He snapped his forehead in a kind of salute. They looked at each other and giggled but accepted. They examined the boxes as they walked off.

"Why don't you carry this thing for a while?" I said.

"Did you see the look on their faces? Let this be a lesson to you"—he started up the street—"to give is to be blessed."

"What's so great about that?" I said, catching up. "Anybody can give away candy."

"But I made two fellow human beings happy. How many have you made happy today?"

I shifted the teddy bear to the other arm. "You just didn't know what to do with those chocolate-covered cherries."

"I made them happy and that's what counts."

"You made their teeth fall out quicker." I had to talk above the noise of rock 'n' roll coming from a music store. "You just made their teeth fall out quicker, that's all."

The airplane man was not paying attention. He

scanned the windows of the various stores we passed. I followed him into a sporting goods store. He twirled a circular rack filled with fishing poles until he found one which interested him. He gave it a couple of whips, then sighted down its length, then replaced it. He tried out another, and another, and another, giving all of them two or three whips through the air, then sighting down them. The salesman pretended to be rearranging some thermal socks, but he had his eye on the airplane man.

"That's a good one," I said. "That's just like mine at home."

"Too stiff."

"Eight ninety-five—a real steal," said the salesman. He looked like a student from the college up the hill. His white shirt was a couple of sizes too big.

The airplane man went through the assortment of rifles, holding each to his cheek, squeezing off shots, the salesman wincing with each click. Finally he bought a hunting knife, which he attached to his belt. The salesman said that was a real steal too. We left the store.

"Part of that knife has to show, you know. Otherwise it's a concealed weapon."

"You think that matters to a fugitive from justice?"

We walked on in silence, out past the sidewalks and blocks, out east where Highway 2 straightens into a strip of drive-ins and car lots and cinder-block businesses. We were both sweating, but still we walked until we were beyond the bowling alley and the lot that sold Half Moon trailers. We stopped across the highway from the slaughterhouse. A column of black smoke tumbled from its single stack. The highway disappeared over a hill before us.

"Pigs," I said. "Once I caught a ride up here with a man who was delivering pigs."

"Is there anything up there?" He pointed to the top of the hill.

"Not that I know of."

"Did you see any back there that interested you?"

"What?"

"Cars, for Chrissake."

"Oh!" I turned around. "Well, that's a different story."

"Pigs, you say." He sounded disgusted.

"What?"

"I'll bet that bear is getting heavy," he said.

"Heavy enough."

"Here—I'll trade you. I don't want to take advantage of you." He took the teddy bear and gave me the three boxes of chocolate-covered cherries. We started back.

"I didn't know you had a daughter," I said. For some reason, the candy made me think of the barmaid from Malta.

"Oh yes—she has a birthmark right here," he said, tapping the left side of his neck.

"Is she good-looking?"

"A regular beauty. I'm going to wrap this bear up and send it to her."

"Does she live around here?" I said.

"Are you joking? Not bloody likely, since her husband's an astronaut."

"Really?"

"Well, he hasn't actually been up yet . . . but they live in Houston. At least that's where I'm sending this bear."

"I was just thinking about that night in Malta . . ."

"Thanks for reminding me."

98

"Remember that barmaid?"

"How could I forget? Lying, vicious little tramp."

"She claimed you knew her—from before."

"Not bloody likely." But he glanced at me.

"But why would she say it if it wasn't true?" I asked.

A semi truck throttled down behind us. The noise of the tires on gravel made us jump to the side. As it passed, the airplane man clamped his hand down on his head, as though he were wearing a hat. The cloud of dust obscured the first part of his sentence. ". . . about the wiles of the world!"

"She knew about your daughter's birthmark," I yelled.

"A lucky guess. Don't you understand? She's after my money."

"Is that what you absconded with?"

"What else?"

"Search me—secret documents, maybe."

He didn't answer.

We stopped at a car lot next to the Ford dealer's. It was full of Cadillacs, Thunderbirds, Pontiacs, Fords, Chevrolets, all washed and polished, windshields, paint and chrome gleaming beneath the afternoon sun. I pointed out a couple that looked good for our purposes, one a white Chrysler with red upholstery, the other a Bonneville with the gearshift in between the seats. The airplane man frowned but said nothing. He kept walking deeper into the lot. I was still in the front row, but I could see him over the tops of the cars, frowning at a blue top.

It was a Ford Falcon and it was blue, faded, dull blue, all over. We leaned against it, studying a small trailer, while the salesman went inside to get the papers. The teddy bear was already sitting on the seat, ready to go.

"I don't know if we'll be able to get this thing off the lot," I said.

The salesman wasn't even happy about selling the car. He laid the papers on the hood and told me to sign in a couple of places. Then he gave me the keys and the airplane man gave him two one-hundreds, a fifty and a ten.

It didn't start. The salesman got a mechanic from the Ford garage who fooled with the wires, took the distributor cap off, then hit the solenoid a couple of times with his screwdriver. Everything seemed to be in working order. The three of them pushed me out onto the gravel shoulder beside the highway, grunting, swearing, building up speed. I popped the clutch and the motor coughed two or three times—then to my everlasting surprise, it caught. I pushed the clutch in and raced the motor, slowing to a stop. The airplane man caught up and heaved himself into the seat. We sat there for a minute while he caught his breath. I clicked on the radio.

"Where are the cherries?" he said.

"Uh-oh." I skipped back to the car lot. They were sitting on the hood of the white Chrysler. The cherries were probably floating in chocolate soup, but I took them back to the car and threw them in the backseat.

I twirled the dials on the radio, then punched the buttons beneath it. I stuck my hand up underneath the dashboard to see if the radio was warm. There was nothing there.

"Well, let's go get a bite—all this exertion has whetted my appetite."

We drove downtown in first gear in order to charge up the battery.

"Pull over beside this hotel."

He took the teddy bear in his arm. I gunned the motor a few times before shutting it off. A cloud of blue smoke seeped in through the back windows.

"She claimed she was your daughter's sister."

He didn't answer.

"She claimed she used to dance for you—you used to give her a dollar to dance."

He opened his door.

"How much money did you abscond with, anyway?"

He entered the hotel. I watched him through the plate-glass window. The clerk handed him his key and a piece of paper, which he looked at intently before bounding up the stairs.

I felt under the dashboard again. The radio just wasn't there. I got out and pushed down the aerial, then leaned against the fender to wait. I glanced up the street, and there she was, the girl who had stolen my gun and electric razor, standing in front of The Silver Dollar. She seemed to be waiting for someone. I ducked back. Even though she was in the middle of the next block, I knew that she would recognize me. Dougie had probably told her that I was looking for her. That would sharpen her eye. I pulled the aerial up again, and there was Dougie standing beside her, pointing in my direction. He took her arm. She shook her head, her short dark hair flaring for an instant. He let her go and walked quickly into The Silver Dollar. There was something almost defiant in the way she stood, feet spread slightly, looking at me, but her short blue dress and short hair made her look bewildered, like a child caught roaming the halls in school. She turned and walked next door to Gable's, glancing back as she opened the door.

I wanted to follow her, to forget about the airplane man and his crazy business, his daughter and the purple teddy bear. I wanted to buy her a drink and sit with her and talk about whatever we had talked about before she stole my gun and electric razor. I wanted to be with her, but I didn't move. I didn't know how to go to her. There were people counting on me to make her suffer, and I too felt that she should suffer a little. Afterwards, I could buy her a drink.

The airplane man had changed clothes. He was wearing a white shirt with a dark blue handkerchief knotted around his neck, a blue-and-white striped sports coat and white pants. He had dusted off his safari boots.

"What do you think?" he said.

"You look like a regular dude."

"That's the ticket, just the sort who would be catching a plane out of Calgary, wouldn't you say?"

"I don't know—that's where the Calgary Stampede is."

"Well, must be a lot of dudes around there. Incidentally, we're going to be delayed—we'll leave at midnight."

We ate a couple of chicken-fried steaks apiece. As the airplane man explained the details of the plan, I experienced a funny feeling of excitement and sadness. If I went through with it, I would become somebody else and the girl would have no meaning for me. Seeing her in front of The Silver Dollar had sparked a warmth in me that surprised me, that I couldn't remember having felt in years. It seemed funny that it should happen now, since I had felt nothing for her when we were living together.

"I have some business to take care of," I said.

"Now? But we should stick together now."

"No, I have to do this thing now. Tell you what—I'll meet you in the Palace Bar at ten. It's just across the street."

But I didn't go directly to Gable's. I needed to walk alone for a while. I crossed to the intersection and walked south down the other main street of Havre. I passed the spot where the airplane man had given the girls the chocolate-covered cherries. A couple of blocks later, I stood in front of a movie house. There was a double feature playing, one Western starring John Wayne, the other Randolph Scott. Both movies looked familiar. They had probably played in every town in Montana once a year for the past twenty. On the billboard, Randolph Scott, dressed in a red double-breasted shirt, white hat and blazing guns, grinned cruelly at me.

The twenty years slipped away and I was a kid again, Mose at my side.

*Do you suppose he shoots as well with his left hand as he does with his right?*

*I'll bet he's plenty fast. Those guys practice.*

*I'm talking about accuracy. Have you ever shot a pistol with your left hand?*

*I can't remember. It would be hard to aim. But, see, he doesn't even have to.*

*I'm talking about handling the gun. You just try it. Maybe he's left-handed.*

*How about his right hand then?*

## 25

Fall had been brief that year. The heavy August days had lazed into September with a heat that denied the regular change of seasons. The days did not become shorter, the nights did not cool off, nor did the stars turn white. It seemed that the hot, fly-buzzing days would never break, that summer would last through Christmas. Mosquitoes swarmed in the evenings outside the kitchen window and redwing blackbirds hid in the ragged cattails of the irrigation ditches.

Then, toward the end of September (when everyone was talking of years past), fall arrived. The leaves of the cottonwoods changed to dusty gold and fell; the fields of alfalfa, long since cut and baled, turned black beneath a black sky that refused to rain. Mosquitoes disappeared one night as if by magic, and the blackbirds flocked up for their flight south. At night the sky cleared off, revealing stars that did not give off light, so that one looked at them with the feeling that he might not be seeing them, but rather some obscure points of white that defied distance, were both years and inches from his nose.

And then it turned winter. Although it had not snowed and no one admitted it, we all felt the bite of winter in our bones. It was during one of those bitter nights that my father, First Raise, who had not even had time to make his plans for the taking of elk in Glacier Park, decided to bring the cows down from their summer range. We had been expecting it, so the announcement came as no great surprise. First Raise said to Mose, "You and your brother bring the cows in tomorrow." Teresa packed a lunch that night—sandwiches and hard-boiled eggs. We went to bed early, not really expecting to do much sleeping but to lie and think of the several places on the range where the cows would be this time of year. Huddled beneath the star quilt, we plotted routes that would allow us to sweep the ravines and reservoirs, the buttes from which we could see the washouts and cutbanks that would shelter the cows from a high wind. In the glass cupboard by the door, the circles of arrowheads, the jackknife and skulls, the coin collection were as distant as the stars.

First Raise woke us up about four in the morning. Without a word he shook Mose awake, then me (but I had been waiting). We dressed quickly—long johns, blue jeans, flannel shirts and boots. As we tiptoed through the living room, my grandmother, who was old even then, watched us without sign of recognition.

First Raise cooked breakfast on the wood stove. He wore a pair of Levi's and a work shirt. He would be fixing machines later in the day. We watched him break the eggs on the side of the frying pan, then jump back as the grease curled the edges black. In another frying pan, he dropped slices of bread into bubbling butter that hissed a keen smell through the kitchen.

First Raise set the plates of food before us. The eggs were yellow and white and black, the bread golden brown. He went over to the bucket beside the washbasin and dipped us each a glass of water, then sat silently watching us eat. The eggs were like rubber. First Raise smiled. It was beginning to get light.

First Raise got us each a cup of coffee and watched us

drink. It was beginning to get light. He loved us. He watched us drink the bitter coffee down. In the living room beside the oil stove, my grandmother snored. Behind the closed door leading off the kitchen, Teresa slept or didn't sleep. First Raise watched us drink the coffee down, then stood.

"Ride the west fence first," he said.

Mose was fourteen.

"Ride the west fence. That's where they were the other day; that's where the grazing is," he said.

I was twelve.

We walked down to the corral. It was beginning to get light as we saddled the horses. Bird, just three years old, sniffed the morning air as I tightened the cinch. Mose saddled up the bay, then swung aboard. First Raise stood in the doorway up at the house and watched us ride out. We waved. He smiled.

The horses were strong beneath us when the first orange appeared on the eastern horizon. We rode out past the alfalfa fields, past the gumbo flats. Mose got down and opened the gate. The horses clattered across the highway, shy of the hard surface and alive in the morning chill. There were no cars.

We rode up the west fence, pushing cows out of ravines and cutbanks. Nearly every one of them had a calf by her side. Things went smoothly, even the bulls cooperating, sauntering easily before us. Occasionally a calf would break from the herd, but one of us would ride it down and bring it back. The wild-eyed roan was dry that year but fell in with the rest of the herd. Like a spinster aunt, she avoided the small kicking calves with outraged dignity.

About midmorning we reached the first reservoir. It

was almost dry, three or four muddy pools providing the cows with water. Mose loped over to a knoll just south of the reservoir from which he could look down into the surrounding ravines. He rode easily atop the bay, kicking it once or twice in the ribs, his straw hat which he had soaked and shaped pulled down low over his ears.

It was beginning to warm up a little, but the cattle just stood beside the reservoir, neither grazing nor drinking. From the southeast the clouds, which came every day now, began to appear over the Bear Paws. Within a couple of hours they would erase the sun, bringing with them not rain but a bitter wind.

From the top of the knoll Mose motioned me to continue pushing the cows east, then dropped out of sight down the other side. I kicked Bird in the ribs and he started the herd, moving from side to side behind them, nipping at a calf which lagged behind. The herd was still small, some twenty cows, most with calves, and the two bulls ambling in the middle.

An hour later, Mose appeared on the south horizon, driving five or six cows with calves. As soon as they saw the others, they broke into a trot and began to call.

Mose fell in beside me. His horse's shoulders and flanks were shiny. "Goddamn baboons," he said.

"Striped-ass green suckers," I said.

He laughed and swatted the wild-eyed cow on the rump with the end of his rope. "I saw three coyotes," he said. "Two of them were pups."

"I wish I had my gun with me," I said. "I'd have blasted them."

"You don't have any shells left."

"I might have a couple you don't know about."

"I might go after those deer I saw the other day."

"There aren't any deer around that slough," I said.

"How come I saw four of them the other day?"

"How come you always see them when nobody else is around? I don't notice anybody else seeing any."

"One of them was a buck, six-pointer."

He handed me a piece of gum. It was Juicy Fruit. I unwrapped it and stuck it in my mouth. It was brittle.

"Anyway I might bring my gun tomorrow," I said.

"That's a laugh—you couldn't hit a bull in the ass with a peashooter. Besides, we aren't coming back, we're going to get them all today."

"How many altogether?"

Mose worked a piece of paper out of his hip pocket. "Seventy-eight cows and four bulls—no, three, not counting that one that got into Rankin's range."

From the southeast I could see the dark shadows of the clouds glide across the tan hills. "You better be right—it's liable to be blizzarding by tomorrow!" And the sun disappeared.

We ate lunch under a cutbank out of the wind.

# 26

Randolph Scott had plugged me dead with a memory I had tried to keep away. I turned back toward the bars. It was almost dark but no stars had come out, not even the evening star; the moon was a pale globe above the post office. The cars filled with teen-agers had begun to circle the downtown blocks. The streetlights suddenly flared, then settled to a steady glow. The dots of the clock above the bank said 8:54.

I crossed the intersection and started for Gable's. I looked back up the block at my Falcon. It crouched beside the curb, all but invisible behind a shiny station wagon. As I turned, my eyes caught the light of the Palace Bar. The airplane man was standing to the side of the open door. I stopped. He was talking to a woman. Although she had her back to me, there was something familiar about her hips. She was dressed up in a yellow pants suit cut narrow at the waist. Her hips swelled under the jacket and tapered into long legs that also looked familiar. Legs can't look familiar, but hips . . . *nice little twitch*—it had to be the barmaid from Malta. What was she doing here? The airplane man put his hand on her shoulder and gestured toward the hotel. Then I saw her face and it was the barmaid. In my mind I saw the hotel room in Malta— *the button between her breasts popping*—she had come to my room. She crossed the street and went into the hotel. The airplane man watched her enter, then turned into the Palace Bar.

I looked back down the street to the spot in front of Gable's where the girl who had stolen my gun and electric razor had been standing that afternoon. I felt the car keys in my pocket. Two of them were identical, a third was shorter with a rounded head. I pulled them out and studied them. There was a white tag hanging from the thin wire ring: "Falcon (move!)." I threw the keys into the air. They landed with a clink in the gutter between two parked cars.

She was sitting at the far end of the bar. It took only a moment to pick her out from the crowd of laughing, yelling Indians. She sat with her legs crossed, holding a cigarette away from her eyes. Her dress was hiked up over her lean brown thighs. Above the din, the juke-box belted out a brave old song:

> From loneliness to a wedding ring
> I played an ace and I won a queen

"How's it going?" I said, and sat down beside her. She looked at me quickly and her eyes were dark.

"You shouldn't have come here," she whispered.

"Don't worry about it," I said. "Do you think I care about that gun?"

She dismissed the gun with a wave of her cigarette. "That's not what I mean."

"I couldn't even find a plug-in for that electric razor. I won it."

A round glass of crème de menthe sat on the bar in front of her. I could almost feel the smoothness of her face with my eyes. Except for a gaunt darkness beneath her cheekbones, she could have been a grade-school girl. Her dress was cut almost to the waist in back, her back as smooth as her face. In the high light, her short straight-cut hair glistened like tar. She ran her finger across her upper lip in a sudden gesture of agitation.

I looked around. "What's going on? How come you're so nervous?" All of a sudden I felt nervous too. My mind fluttered back to the airplane man and his plot. I began to suspect that she was in on it.

But she was worried about something else. "Dougie and a couple of his friends are going to beat you up," she whispered.

I looked at her lips and nodded my head stupidly, expecting her to say something real, but she didn't. I looked into her eyes to see if she was serious and she was. The roof of my mouth went dry and my tongue came away from it with a clack. "But what for?"

"He thinks you're looking for him; that's what you're doing here, so he's going to beat you to it."

My expression must have amused her. She smiled. Her teeth were green from the crème de menthe.

"Where is he now?"

"Looking for you. He wants to take you by surprise." Her tone was sympathetic but impersonal. "I don't like it," she said. "I believe in a fair fight."

"Thanks."

"I tried to talk him out of it, you know. I hate that kind of thing." She sounded like an adult, but then she said: "Have you missed me?"

"Where do you think he is now?"

She dropped her shoulders in irritation and sipped at her drink.

I glanced around behind me. Three women were standing in front of the jukebox, looking at the selections and moving their hips to a slow number. One was barefoot. Her feet were flat.

"Look," I said, "maybe I ought to get out of here. We could go someplace else. I have a car now." Then I remembered I had thrown the keys in the gutter. I stood and started for the door.

"Just take it easy—" She held her hands a few inches off the bar and moved them up and down. "Just relax. He just left; he won't be back for a while." She crossed her legs toward me and the blue dress fell further back on her thighs. Although she was very slender, almost bony, her thighs were long and silky. They were the best part of her. So I sat down again, with my back to the bar.

"That's a new dress," I said.

Her green teeth danced in the light. "Do you like it?"

"It's pretty nice. You fill it out pretty well. There isn't much to it, though," I said, looking at her naked back.

"Do you blame me? It's hot."

"Maybe if you settled down you wouldn't be so hot." She ignored my remark. "I don't like violence," she said.

"I'm not exactly in love with it." I glanced around the room again, half expecting Dougie to sneak up on me, but the scene remained unchanged. Two men sat in a booth with their arms around each other. They seemed sad about something. One of the women at the jukebox was scolding them. She hawked a mouthful of spit at them which landed on the table. One of them raised a drunken arm in an attempt to ward off whatever she had in reserve. But she turned back to the jukebox, her hips bouncing to the music.

I whirled around and ordered a couple of crèmes de menthe. My hands were shaking. I couldn't tell if it was fear or love or lust.

"Why don't you settle down?" I said to my hands.

"Pay up," said the bartender. He had thin yellow hair.

When he had left, I said, "If you settled down you'd be a lot better off; you'd be happier, believe me, Agnes."

"You bore me," she said.

"You should learn a trade, shorthand," I said. "There's a crying demand for secretaries."

She looked at me as if she didn't recognize me. "Shorthand?" she squealed.

"Yes, you're young. I was talking to a woman; it's a good living . . ."

"Shorthand," she whispered to her drink.

"It's essential."

I wanted to feel good but something was holding me back. I wasn't afraid anymore. Without announcement, a feeling of resignation had crept into my chest. I was calm, but I didn't feel good. Maybe it was a kind of love. My hands had quit shaking. In the thick light, I couldn't see any hairs on the backs of them. For some reason, this embarrassed me.

"What's the matter with you?" She removed one of her white graduation shoes and shook a pebble out of it.

"I'm not happy, Agnes."

"That's a good one. Who is?"

I hid my hands. "Aren't you?"

She looked puzzled. In her black eyes, I could see the reason I had brought her home that time before. They held the promise of warm things, of a spirit that went beyond her miserable life of drinking and screwing and men like me.

I touched her ribs. "Let's leave here," I said.

Her eyes shifted slightly and the depth went out of them.

"But I have a car," I said. "We could go anywhere, Great Falls—"

Suddenly a hand grabbed my shoulder and whirled me around. In the split second that it happened, I could see frozen beyond the plane of knuckles the sad faces of the men in the booth.

## 27

The wind whistled above the cutbank as Mose and I ate the sandwiches and hard-boiled eggs that Teresa had prepared the night before.

"It'll probably be blizzarding by tomorrow," I said.

"Don't worry. We're over half already and I'll bet the rest are down in that coulee by the west fence."

"I don't feel like moving now. I'm comfortable right where I am," I said.

We both had our sheepherder's coats buttoned to the neck.

"Well, I don't know about you," Mose said, standing and brushing off the seat of his pants, "but I want to get home before dark."

"I'll flip you to see who gets that last egg."

"Go ahead—I've had two already."

We gathered up the rest of them that afternoon. Only one cow was missing, and since it didn't seem likely that she would be on the range by herself, we figured that she had gotten through the fence and was in a neighboring range. Like the bull, she would winter with somebody else's herd.

"What did I tell you," Mose said, as we drove the herd south down to the valley.

"Do you think First Raise will want us to find that other cow?"

"How can we? Unless we ride all the other ranges. That would take us the rest of our lives."

"Do you think First Raise will go on his hunting trip this fall?"

"No."

"I'm going to buy some more bullets tomorrow," I said.

"I'm going after that big buck. Maybe I'll stuff his head."

"As if you know how."

"I can do it," Mose said. He swatted a bull with his rope. "Hi, get moving, you whiteface shittails!"

"You goddamn horse turds," I yelled above the wind.

We had the cattle loping headlong down into the valley, the wild-eyed spinster leading the way.

## 28

"Are you all right?" she said.

I was sitting on the sidewalk, my back against a parking meter. I looked around. Everything came strange as though I were seeing things in slow motion, but nothing moved except my head. A woman knelt beside me. Two children leaning out a car window at the curb stared at me in silence.

"Your tooth is busted," she said. "You come flying out of there like I don't know what—only backwards."

"Which one," I said.

"That one there," she said, pointing at Gable's.

"No . . . I mean, which tooth?"

"That one there," she said, pointing at my mouth. "You must have been feeling awfully good to go in there and raise hell."

I felt the jagged edge of the tooth with my tongue. Blood was beginning to cake on my upper lip.

"Your nose is kind of puffy too—other than that you

don't look so bad." She glanced up at the car behind me. "Well, what the hell are you kids looking at?"

The boy, about five or six, stuck a finger in his nose and continued to stare. His sister began to cry.

"What's your name?" I asked my nurse.

"Marlene." She smiled for the first time.

"My head feels wet . . . are you sure I'm not bleeding?"

"It must be draining down inside your brain." She stood and stepped back. "You need a drink?"

She wore a man's short-sleeve shirt with the sleeves rolled over her upper arms. The shirt strained against her breasts and belly, but she had a pleasant, almost pretty face. She smiled again, showing teeth blackened around the edges.

"Not in there," I said.

"No, hell no." She giggled. "I'll get us something."

I felt the back of my head. "Are you buying?"

"If you give me some money." She laughed again, a girlish twitter that didn't seem possible for her bulk.

I ran my tongue over the busted tooth—it was one of the big front ones—then handed her a five-dollar bill. "Listen, Marlene, you be sure and come back," I said.

## 29

I waited for fifteen or twenty minutes.

For fifteen or twenty minutes the boy in the car stared at me. The girl had lost interest and was trying to turn the steering wheel. She made bubbling noises with her mouth. She pulled the wheel one way, then the other, in an effort to make the tires turn. Either out of frustration or boredom she began to cry again, a controlled sobbing without sound or tears which made her small body tremble. The boy remained unmoved when she snuggled close to him, resting her head against his shoulder. Presently she slept.

The boy did not smile when I held out the quarter. He simply opened his hand.

I walked up the street to where I had tossed the keys. They were still there. I picked them up and walked on.

The man who had torn up his airplane ticket was gone by the time I reached the Palace Bar. There was not a clue that he had been there. I walked into the bathroom and washed up. There was no towel or mirror. I dried my face with toilet paper, gingerly feeling the puffiness on either side of the bridge of my nose. I couldn't tell if my eyes were black.

I ordered a shot of bar whiskey and downed it in a single motion. I almost threw it back up, but it helped to dim the memory of a blow I hadn't seen coming. I ordered another. "You look like you've seen some taller grass, partner," the bartender said. He jerked his thumb at me and winked at another customer. Randolph Scott.

"Hey, Warren," a man called from the doorway, "something seems to be going on out here."

The bartender ambled down to the window. He was wiping a glass. "Ah, hell, probably picking up one of them transvestites . . ."

The customer giggled.

"Nope, I don't think so, Warren. There was a man with a shiny suit who went in with them."

"Another one of them morphodykes from the college . . ."

"Oh, that Warren," a woman exclaimed next to me.

"Nope, I think they mean business this time, Warren."

I stood up on the rungs of my barstool. A red light was flashing across the street.

Customers began to move toward the door.

"Probably one of them pisswillies from up the hill . . ."

"That Warren!" She seemed pleased.

I joined the people at the door. Then I slipped through and stood on the sidewalk. There was a crowd of people in the big square of light in front of the hotel. I broke into a trot until I reached the perimeter of the crowd.

"What's going on?" I asked.

Nobody answered. They were pressing forward, trying to see into the windows of the hotel.

"What are they doing?" I said.

All the faces were yellow from the light above them.

I skirted the crowd, first to the left, then to the right, trying to get closer. I came back to the police car in the street. Two men were leaning against the trunk. One had a camera.

"Who are they arresting?" I said.

"Search me," said the one without the camera.

"How should we know?" said the other.

"I just arrived," said the first one. "I'm with the newspaper."

"But you must have heard something . . ."

"They just sent me out here."

"We're not mind readers," said the second. He was fooling with his camera.

I pressed into the crowd again, but it was hopeless. I returned to the newspapermen.

"Here he comes again."

"Don't look at us."

Their insistence irritated me.

"I might know who it is . . ." I began.

"Go on, how could you?"

"The devil with you!"

Another police car arrived. It was the highway patrol. As the officer passed us, one of the newspapermen touched him on the shoulder. "What's going on, officer? We're from the paper . . ." The officer looked at the hand on his shoulder. He began to wade through the crowd. "Look out there, step back, all of you, clear the area!"

The first newspaperman looked at me suspiciously. "Who do you think it is?"

"Yeah," jeered the second.

It was after I opened my mouth that I realized I had never learned his name. "Well, he's big—"

Suddenly the crowd grew silent and parted before us. The airplane man, handcuffed, walked between a policeman and the man in the shiny suit. The policeman waved the hunting knife that we had bought that day. The shiny suit carried a small plaid suitcase. Behind them, the highway patrolman carried the purple teddy bear. He muttered, "Step back."

I began to back up, out of the perimeter of light, when the airplane man spotted me. A quick chill ran through my scalp. He said something. I moved forward a couple of steps.

"What happened to your nose?" he said.

Then he was in the backseat of the police car and it was moving. I realized that I was standing beside the Falcon. The three boxes of chocolate-covered cherries lay on the backseat.

"What did happen to your nose?" said the first newspaperman. He had a pad and pencil at the ready.

## 30

I sat in front of the hotel. On the one hand, I wanted to start up the Falcon and drive home; on the other, I wanted to see the barmaid from Malta. I didn't know why, but I was sure she was still in the hotel hiding out until the coast was clear. I had no idea which room she was in and the desk clerk wouldn't help even if I knew her name. Again I felt that helplessness of being in a world of stalking white men. But those Indians down at Gable's were no bargain either. I was a stranger to both and both had beaten me.

I should go home, I thought, turn the key and drive home. It wasn't the ideal place, that was sure, but it was the best choice. Maybe I had run out of choices.

So I sat and waited. An hour went by, then two, but still no barmaid from Malta. I got out of the car and walked up to the big window of the hotel. The desk clerk was bent over a magazine. The lobby was yellow and empty.

I found Marlene wandering around with two six-packs of beer. She said she had been looking for me, but she looked surprised to see me. She held the sack in both arms as though she were carrying groceries home from Safeway.

"You should see yourself," she said.

We took a room in a gray hotel down by the railroad station. The elevator man was as gray as the green walls. He said the elevator was out of order.

"Why do you exist then?" I said.

"To take people up and down, whichever way they want to go," said the gray man.

Marlene and I sat on the edge of the bed and drank a couple of beers. Every time she looked at me, her eyes watered. She said it was because of my own swollen eyes. Finally I laid her back on the bed and unzipped her pants.

I never left the softness of her body. The first light of dawn caught me draped over her belly, my chin in the hollow of her shoulder, my eyes staring at a coarse black hair on the white pillow. A rectangle of sun began to spread across the bed, framing our bodies for no one to see. Marlene stirred. I pinched her nostrils together and a great rasp began in her throat. Then her small black eyes were open.

"Kiss my pussy," she said gently.

I touched her lips with my finger. "Kiss your ass, my great brown hump."

She smiled and wrapped her arms around me. Her breath was warm and pleasant like a child's. Once again I rooted in the heat of her.

When I awoke the second time, the sun was around midmorning. The room smelled of beer and sweat, familiar, and Marlene. I disentangled myself and sat up. A vacuum cleaner hummed from somewhere far away. I found a full can of beer among the empties on the nightstand and opened it. A quick sip and the smell made me put it down.

Marlene lay on her back, mouth open and legs closed tight. Her hips were narrow for her bulk; her breasts lay small and soft on her chest, but her belly rose taut and shiny. I placed my palm against it and pushed; when I drew my hand back it sprang out like an inner tube.

Her shirt lay over a chairback next to the bed. Several cigarettes had spilled from the pack in her pocket and lay on the seat. I lit one up and coughed out a cloud of smoke. A rush of dizziness filled my head. When I closed my eyes a swarm of tiger tails appeared, and blue dots, millions of them, flickered. I fell back against her thigh.

From somewhere came the muffled sound of a guitar, a quiet strum that had no tune. It seemed an unlikely place, an unlikely time, but there was no mistaking the monotony that kept a man company. He began to sing. "If you loved me . . ." Then he stopped altogether. After a long pause, he started over. "If you loved me half as much as I love you . . ." There was another pause, then: "You wouldn't stay . . . you wouldn't stay . . . you wouldn't stay away half as much . . ." The guitar thrummed violently, followed by a brittle clatter like a chair being knocked over.

Marlene sighed and tried to roll over, but the pressure of my head held her in place. She drew another breath, held it, then let it out at once, a quick gasp, and the regular up-and-down rhythm of her belly resumed.

I sat up and looked at her. A kind of pity rose within me. Her naked body seemed so vulnerable, so innocent, that I wanted to cover her with my own. I touched her knee and she spread her legs. The sound of traffic in the street below became a roar. I closed my eyes and saw the barmaid from Malta, the button between her breasts popping, Malvina, the bubble-bath globes scattered among the perfumes, the girl who had stolen my gun, her short blue dress, standing defiantly, helplessly, on the sidewalk . . .

I dropped the cigarette into the ashtray and covered Marlene, burrowing down into her, trying to disappear into her flesh—it was not enough, not good. I wanted her to be alive. I straddled her, resting my butt against her belly. I kissed her on the neck, on the ear, on the nose. I shook her, tickled her, kneaded her breasts.

"Kiss my pussy," she murmured, and I slapped her hard across the cheek.

Her head jerked from the pillow almost as quickly as I had slapped her. Her eyes were flat and round. "What did you do that for?" she cried. "Jesus Christ!" The muscles in her neck stood out as she strained to keep her head up. Her arms were pinned beneath my knees. "What kind of sonofabitch are you, anyway?"

I sat back. I could feel the belly muscles working beneath me as she flailed her legs. Beyond that she couldn't move. In one tremendous effort she tried to roll me off, but I sat, grave as a stone, on her belly. "If only I could get loose, you dirty bastard, if only . . ."—her voice strained and muffled against her teeth.

Suddenly her head collapsed against the pillow and her body went limp. My butt sank into her belly. She turned her head and sobbed, "If only I could get loose," and I thought of the little girl of the night before, her frustration, her brother and his blank yet curious stare. And I was staring at the sobbing woman with the same lack of emotion, the same curiosity, as though I were watching a bug floating motionless down an irrigation ditch, not yet dead but having decided upon death.

I slid off her. Everything had gone out of me, and I felt the kind of peace that comes over one when he is alone, when he no longer cares for warmth, or sunshine, or possessions, or even a woman's body, so yielding and powerful.

I began to put on my clothes. The sobbing stopped.

I buttoned my pants, then sat on the edge of the bed to slip into my shoes. For the first time I noticed how old they looked, run-down and run-over, the cat holding his paw up barely eyeing me from the one which lay upside down under the bed.

Marlene sat up, holding the pillow against her belly, one breast exposed and staring past the roundness of her middle. Her knees were raised beneath the sheet and together.

"And you're going to leave just like that," she said.

I tied my shoelaces.

"Did you pay for this room?"

I nodded.

"Have you got some money for me?" She added shyly: "It's okay if you don't."

I pulled some loose bills out of my pocket and began to count them. I dropped them on the bed. "It's all I have."

"You could come back."

I opened the door. "I might."

"You could stay and maybe we could talk for a while."

I turned. Her shirt had fallen off the chair. Her blue jeans lay on the floor by the nightstand, panties still in them. I looked at Marlene. The pillow covered her belly, her breast studied the sheet. She had drawn her legs up so that the nipple was only inches from its object. The face was the same face that had looked into mine when I sat with my back against the parking meter in front of Gable's. I avoided her eyes because they too would be the same.

## 31

I had had enough of Havre, enough of town, of walking home, hung over, beaten up, or both. I had had enough of the people, the bartenders, the bars, the cars, the hotels, but mostly, I had had enough of myself. I wanted to lose myself, to ditch these clothes, to outrun this burning sun, to stand beneath the clouds and have my shadow erased, myself along with it.

I traced the hump of my nose with a fingernail. It was very tender, and swollen, so that it was almost a straight plane from the bridge to the cheekbones. I walked down the street, out past the car lots, the slaughterhouse, away from Havre. There were no mirrors anywhere.

# Part Three

## 32

The big smooth-riding Oldsmobile streaked down the highway, floating over bumps like a duck on the wind-whipped slough beside the corral. The man and his wife in the front seat spoke about the countryside as if it were dead, as if all life had become extinct. Occasionally she would point at something, a shack or a busted-down corral beside an irrigation ditch, and he would nod and roar excitedly. His great black beard and shaggy head made him look rugged, but behind the sideburns his ears stuck out, white and delicate. A black hat with a rounded crown and straight brim sat on his head. He looked like a Hutterite. His wife wore a beaded leather band around her neck.

His questions entered my mind as part of the drone of the motor. Only the way he looked at the rearview mirror made me realize that he was talking to me. Sometimes I asked him to repeat the question; other times I said yes or no, never fully understanding what he wanted to know. My confusion, after a time, left him to his own thoughts and his wife's magnetic finger.

The daughter sat in the backseat with me, a case of peaches separating us. She was a frail girl with skin as white as the man's ears. Her own ears were hidden beneath a flow of black frizzled hair contained by a blue-and-white beaded headband. She lolled back in the corner, sometimes looking at me, sometimes gazing blankly out the window at the unchanging country. At first, her grunts seemed to be in agreement with whatever her parents were talking about, but then she grunted twice during a lull in the conversation. She seemed to be in some kind of discomfort. Her eyes were dull, like those of a sick calf.

The sudden slowing of the car jarred me awake. We pulled off the highway onto a dirt road and stopped. Before the man could shut the motor off, the girl was out and running. She disappeared behind a stand of chokecherry bushes.

"It's the water," the man said. "She's quite delicate."

"This is White Bear," I said. "My house is five miles down the highway."

"She has pills but she neglects them," said the wife. "She's never been healthy."

"Good health is of prime importance," I said. "Maybe I could walk from here."

"Nonsense. In this heat? Don't be absurd."

The water in the reservoir was low, three feet below

the lip of the dam. Cattails on either side were turning ragged.

"Are there any fish in there?" asked the man.

"Turtles," I said.

"Do you Indians eat them?"

The girl came out from behind the chokecherry bushes. If she were any paler from vomiting you couldn't tell. She seemed to be shivering and her hands were thrust into the pockets of her shorts. She smiled shyly as she got into the car. She was very pretty. A piece of red hung from the point of her chin.

I smiled back at her and a sudden pain shot up through my swollen nose.

"How do you feel, honey?" asked the wife, but before I could answer, the girl said fine, and the waters of White Bear whispered to the sun.

The man let me off opposite the road into the ranch, saying to be sure and look them up if I ever got to Michigan, saying he really meant it, he was a professor. The daughter handed me a peach wrapped in crinkly purple paper. I thanked her, and him, and the wife, and waved, and walked down the incline.

"Can I take your picture?"

"Yes," I said, and stood beside a gatepost. He pointed a small gadget at me; then he turned a couple of knobs on the camera, held it to his face and clicked.

## 33

I threw a clod of gumbo into the rosebush. Nothing happened. I picked up another and threw it. This time

I heard something scurry to the other end. I began to pelt the rosebush until a hen pheasant lifted, whirring low over the gumbo flat to an alfalfa field, where she landed and entered the weeds of a ditch.

A hundred yards further, where the ditch joined another, I saw the tall, old cottonwood. Its limbs were almost bare, just a few twigs where the leaves still hung. One of its branches had broken off and lay near the spot where the hawk had fallen. Even Mose had had to admit it was a good shot. Resting the .22 on the wheel of an old hay wagon, I squeezed the trigger the way First Raise had shown me, exhaling, a steady pressure and *bang!* the hawk tumbled down in an erratic spin. He gained his feet as soon as he hit the ground. Mose and I ran whooping and stumbling through the plowed field. We stopped a few feet short of the tree. The hawk squatted low to the ground, his wings spread for balance, the tips of them brushing the weeds, yellow eyes alert, flashing. He bent his head forward and opened his beak to reveal a small pale tongue. He seemed to be hissing at us although he made no sound. The feathers on his breast were red and matted.

It must have been the tongue. We had not considered that a hawk might have a tongue. It seemed too personal, private, even human. The hawk opened his beak wider, the tongue moved slightly, then the head grew heavier and began to sink. We stood motionless, quiet, and watched him die. The weeds held him in the position he had taken up after falling, but his head lay limp on his breast, the feathers on his neck ruffled and jutting toward the sky. I ejected the spent shell and turned, but Mose had already walked away.

I threw the purple paper in a clump of sagebrush and

began to eat the peach. It tasted bitter, like metal on my tongue, but I ate it, partly because I hadn't eaten anything that day, but, more, out of loyalty toward the sick girl.

The sun was low over the slough by the time I walked into the yard. Although I had only been gone for a couple of days, a weariness had settled in my bones. I hadn't even drunk much, except for the night with Malvina. Damn her, I might have stayed with her and avoided all the trouble later.

The water in the drinking bucket was warm. The tin dipper floated on the surface. Lame Bull and Teresa were not around. The old lady was gone too. Her rocking chair stood empty and dark in the darkening living room. The seat where her thin butt had rested was shiny, the bar across the top of the back greasy where her head had lain. The movie magazines piled beside the other chair were gone. I rocked the old lady's chair a couple of times. It didn't squeak. I glanced around the room. For the first time in my life, I was able to look at the room without the feeling that I was invading my grandmother's privacy. But now I saw that almost nothing in the room belonged to her, just the rocker and the cot next to the oil stove. The blankets were neatly folded and piled on top of each other. The star quilt was also folded. A pillow, without a pillowcase, rested on the blankets. The old lady must have died. That's why the house was so quiet. I dropped down into the rocker, then stood again, quickly. I walked to the window and opened the shade. Perhaps it was the suggestion of death, but I smelled it, dark and musty, as surely as one smells the mother's milk in the breath of a baby.

The tobacco pouch hung by a thong from the rocker

arm. I untied it and brought it to the window. It was as soft as old Bird's muzzle. I squeezed it and felt the arrowhead inside. Besides the two pieces of furniture, this pouch and the clothes on her back, I had never seen any of the old lady's possessions, but she must have had other things, things that would have been buried with her in the old days. Now, almost a hundred years later, she would be buried the way she was born, with nothing.

I walked into the kitchen and turned on the white plastic radio on top of the refrigerator. The room, with its two windows on the sun side, was still bright and hot. I tuned in Great Falls, then turned on the electric stove. I got the galvanized tub from the shed, poured the water from the drinking bucket into it and set it on the burner. Teresa never used the wood stove anymore, but I thought of First Raise cooking breakfast on it, frying eggs and bread. He would have been surprised to see the electric stove next to it. I filled another bucket from the cistern, then began to undress. I hadn't noticed the bloodstains on my shirt before—there were five of them, one after another, down the front. I opened a burner plate on the wood stove and stuffed it in.

With a hot pad on each handle, I lifted the tub from the electric stove to the floor. Steam rolled from the surface of the shallow water. Sunday nights Mose and I used to bathe in the tub on the kitchen floor, in the same water, until it turned the gray of the metal tub. That was a different kind of dirt—dust from the roads, chaff from the hayfields—not the invisible kind that coats a man who has been to town. I poured from the drinking bucket into the tub until the water became lukewarm to my hand. Because of my bad leg I could not squat, so I hunched over from the waist and began to scrub myself. Music filled the kitchen as I ran the soapy washrag over my body. It was good to be home. The weariness I had felt earlier vanished from my bones.

I lifted the drinking bucket above my head and tilted it. I caught my breath as the water poured over my body into the tub and onto the floor. I almost lost my balance, rocking the tub on its battered bottom. I pulled a chair over from the kitchen table and sat down, my feet still in the dirty water. I had forgotten the towel, but the sun was low enough so that its rays spread across the kitchen. I listened to the music, and, at six o'clock, the stock report out of Chicago. Then I went into Teresa's bedroom and searched through her ironing until I found a clean shirt, underwear and pants.

After emptying the tub and mopping the floor, I walked down to the corral to feed the calf. Bird and the red horse were in the small pasture behind the corral with the calf's mother. They all watched me with interest.

## 34

"She passed away," Teresa said, setting down the sack of groceries.

"What did you do to your nose?" Lame Bull said.

Teresa looked at him. "It was a merciful death."

"No, seriously, what did you do to your nose?"

"Where is she now?" I said.

"We took her to Harlem." Teresa began to put the canned goods in the cupboard.

"Somebody busted me one," I said to Lame Bull. "How come? Why don't we just bury her here, where the rest of them are?"

"She was a fine woman," Lame Bull said.

"Because they have to fix her up. They'll make her look nice. And Father Kittredge will want to say a few words over her."

"But it would have been easier to bury her here," I said. "She didn't even go to church."

"Can't you get it through your head that we *are* going to bury her here?" The voice was calm. "As for looking nice—it's the least we can do."

"Standard procedure," Lame Bull said.

"Will the priest come down to bury her?"

Teresa turned. She had been putting the milk in the icebox. "I don't know, if he can get away."

"Like he did when we stuck First Raise in the ground?"

She looked away. "He's very busy. They're sending him to another parish . . . Idaho."

"Look here, boy." Lame Bull pulled a bottle of wine from a paper sack.

I couldn't help myself. "I don't think anybody I know is going to miss him."

Teresa reacted as though the words had no particular meaning for her. She took three glasses from the cupboard and set them on the table.

"At least nobody on this reservation . . . maybe a few of his friends in Harlem."

Again, nothing. But there was something different about her face. She had always had a clear bitter look, not without humor, that made the others of us seem excessive, too eager to talk too much, drink too much,

134

breathe too fast. Now, solemnity had darkened her eyes. As she bent over the table, I saw, perhaps because my grandmother was gone, how much she had come to resemble the old lady.

"I know how it is," Lame Bull said. "What we all need is a glass of wine. That'll pick us right up."

Teresa sat at the other end of the table. I handed a glass to her. The kitchen was beginning to get dark. In the momentary silence, I could hear the high whine of the mosquitoes as they gathered outside the window screens.

I picked up my glass and took a swallow of wine.

"What do you think? I want your opinion."

"Okay."

"Ho! Okay he says." He pulled the bottle closer. "V-i-n R-o-s-e. How do you say that?"

"I don't know. Vin Rose, I guess."

He lifted the bottle and sniffed. "I saw a guy drinking this once in Great Falls." He screwed the cap down.

Teresa hadn't touched her wine. She seemed to be listening to the mosquitoes, or thinking about her mother, or the priest.

"Oh, I know how it is—you're young, you take things seriously, you get older, you buy a bottle of good wine, you drink to those who are still living." He raised his glass. "Me, I'm still ticking, so I drink to all of us, all my loved ones."

In spite of myself, I raised my glass.

Teresa stood and walked quickly into the bedroom. The door shut with a soft click.

Lame Bull looked surprised. He still had his glass in his hand.

The bedsprings groaned once and it was quiet.

"I know what it is—that fool priest and then that bloodsucker down at the funeral parlor." He sighed and opened a bag of Fritos. Then, as if he hadn't the energy to eat them, he pushed the bag away.

We sat silently in the darkening kitchen. The mosquitoes continued to whine. The yellow of the radio dial illuminated the refrigerator. There was no music, only the buzzing of electricity from the depths of the cabinet.

"Have some Fritos, pal—we got us a grave to dig tomorrow."

## 35

Digging the grave was easy. Lame Bull operated the spud bar and I the shovel. The bar sank easily into the brown earth, loosening great dry clods which I flung out of the hole. Although we had started early enough, by ten o'clock we were stripped to the waist and sweating. My handkerchief, which I had tied around my forehead, was soaked. But it was easy work, not like the winter we had planted First Raise. With two bars and a fifth of whiskey, we had struggled through three feet of frozen ground, chipping it like flakes off an arrowhead. By nightfall we still hadn't worked our way through the frost. The snow around the hole was littered with chips of earth. Early the next morning, Lame Bull's bar broke through. He struck with such fury that the bar sank half its length and we had to chip it out with the other one. An hour later we had the hole dug, squared off and the coffin in place. Instead of any feeling of sorrow for my dead father, I felt only relief that we had finally gotten the hole dug. The sorrow, what there was of it, came later.

Lame Bull wanted to dig my grandmother's grave five feet long because that was how long she was. He was willing to add a couple of inches at each end in case she had grown any in the funeral parlor. But I convinced him that her coffin would probably be as large as any, so we made it another foot longer. By way of compromise, we only dug it down to five feet. But it was a good five feet, squared off nicely, the base as level as a tabletop and the dirt piled neatly on the side.

We sat on the pile to rest. Lame Bull rolled a smoke, which we passed back and forth. Across the hole I noticed that First Raise's grave had sunk about a foot. Although surrounded by weeds, the grave itself was bare, except for a Styrofoam cross with two dirty plastic flowers tied to it. I couldn't tell what they were supposed to represent. They were white with yellow feelers coming out of their centers.

A rectangular piece of granite lay at the head of the grave. On it were written the name, John First Raise, and a pair of dates between which he had managed to stay alive. It said nothing about how he had liked to fix machines and laugh with the white men of Dodson, or how he came to be frozen stiff as a plank in the borrow pit by Earthboy's.

Teresa waved a scarf from the doorway of the shed. From this distance she looked big and handsome, clean-featured, unlike the woman I had seen the night before. She was wearing a white blouse and red pants. It must have been cool in the house, for she was wearing a sweater over the blouse. The white scarf followed the arc of her arm back and forth above her head. When we stood up, it disappeared and Teresa disappeared back into the house.

Lame Bull threw the cigarette butt in the hole. "I don't see why they can't just bring her down here like your old man."

"Teresa has to make arrangements."

"What's wrong with doing that after we get the old lady in the ground?"

"He likes his money in advance—otherwise he'll keep her in cold storage." I jumped down into the hole and stamped on the cigarette.

"How much?"

"I don't know, two, three hundred. We had to borrow money to get First Raise out."

"Jumping Jesus! You mean all that for a coffin?"

"No, hell—you heard Teresa. They'll make her up, put some lipstick and rouge on her, new dress maybe." I nudged some dirt on the cigarette, then stamped it flat.

Lame Bull put his shirt on.

"It isn't cheap," I said.

He buttoned the buttons deliberately. "That funeral parlor has one hell of a job on their hands."

I watched him walk off toward the house. His shirttail covered his behind. Before he reached the house, he stopped and looked off toward the corral, then the tool-shed. He turned and glanced at a stack of bales in the alfalfa field to the east. He seemed to be surveying his property to make sure today and tomorrow would be worth it.

I climbed out of the hole.

It was going to be hot again, but from the southeast a few puffy white clouds were beginning to build up.

It was hard to tell if they were coming toward the ranch. More likely they would sweep south over the Little Rockies. There was little chance of rain—it was the time of year when things grow stagnant, each morning following blue on the heels of the last, the sun rising, circling, falling day after day. Not like fall, I thought, with its endless gray, a time of dusk, with wind that cuts through your clothes and your skin, through the meat of you, until it reaches your bones, where it lodges itself. Not like fall, when the cold walks with you and beds down with you at night, never leaving you except for those couple of hours in the evening when the oil stove hums it out of your bones. A damned, ugly cold. Fall into winter.

We shouldn't have run them, I thought, it wasn't good for them—

## 36

But it was getting dark and we still had to get them across the highway. So we had them racing full tilt down the hill into the valley, both of us swearing and swatting at their behinds with the end of our ropes. The wild-eyed spinster was stretched flat-out, running low to the ground like some ungainly antelope which the others chased. Behind them came the bulls, their short legs almost a blur in the dusk, their heads swinging from side to side, hooking the wind, and the bucking calves, the white of their faces, necks and underbellies almost dead white.

Down in the valley they slowed to a trot, and Mose loped around them to open the gates.

I had lost track of the cold in our wild rush down the hill, but now as we trotted across the valley floor toward the highway, I felt the wind sing through my clothes. The tops of my thighs were numb beneath the worn Levi's and long johns. Tears rolled back away from my eyes.

Mose skirted the cows and rode up beside me. He wiped his nose with his coat sleeve.

"Okay, we've got to keep them moving—through this gate, over the highway and down through the other gate. Got that?" He tried to sound confident. "We've got to keep them moving. Okay?"

"Roger," I said.

Mose was fourteen.

It should have been easy. All of the cows had been through the routine before. They knew that when the weather turned cold and the sky gray, it was time to come in. After grazing the dry prairie grass, they were anxious to get at the alfalfa and bluejoint stubble.

It was dusk, that time of day the light plays tricks on you, when you think you can see better than you actually can, or see things that aren't there. The time of day your eyes, ears, nose become confused, all become one gray blur in the brain, so you step outside your body and watch the movie of a scene you have seen before. So it seemed, as I cut back and forth behind the herd, that I was somewhere else, not far, a hawk circling above or a beetle tracing corridors in the earth below the stamping hooves.

We pushed them through the first gate, up the incline and onto the highway. Screaming and swearing, we flailed at the stragglers with the ends of our ropes. The cows clattered on the hard surface of the highway, milling, circling, shying. My eyes watered in the gray wind until Mose seemed a crystal motion, no more or less distinct than the smell of fresh crap or the squeak of leather. The cows were spooked by the sound of their own hooves on the unfamiliar asphalt. The bulls swayed behind them, tensely, waiting to see which way the herd would move. We struck at them, but they wouldn't move without a direction.

Suddenly the spinster raced headlong down the incline. The other cows plunged after her and the bulls began to lumber across the highway.

It should have been easy. All we had to do was get them through the gate, close it and push them back a ways, away from the highway. Then we could go home to a plateful of meat and potatoes, and drink hot coffee, and tell First Raise all about it. He would listen and be pleased that we had done our job, surprised that we had done it in one day. And he would tell us how to be smart, how he had charged the white man from Dodson twenty dollars to kick his baler awake, "One dollar for the kick . . ." By now the light was almost gone and these thoughts were as real to me as the cows bunched up on the incline.

But the spinster wouldn't go through the gate. She stopped before it and lowered her head. I could see only the bulk of her back in front of the others, but in my movie I saw how she was standing, legs spread and stiff, head cocked to one side, the skin on her shoulders rippling in spasms as though she were trying to shake off a horsefly.

It was at this instant that I felt Bird quiver beneath me and gather his weight in his hindquarters. Then I saw the small shape of a calf break from the herd. I barely had time to grab the saddle horn before Bird leaped forward, chasing the calf along the fence line. We stayed on the shoulder of the highway, keeping the calf between the barbed wire and us. Mose yelled but I couldn't stop. With one hand I pushed with all my strength against the saddle horn; with the other I pulled back on the reins until I was standing, my legs stiff against the stirrups which were forward around Bird's shoulders. I couldn't raise his head, I had no strength, and so I clung helplessly to the horn.

Through a prism of tears I saw the searching yellow lights, the gray whine of metal, and it was past me, a scream of air whipping the hat off my head, the stinging blast against my face.

I couldn't have seen it—we were still moving in the opposite direction, the tears, the dark and wind in my eyes—the movie exploded whitely in my brain, and I saw the futile lurch of the car as the brake lights popped, the horse's shoulder caving before the fender, the horse spinning so that its rear end smashed into the door, the smaller figure flying slowly over the top of the car to land with the hush of a stuffed doll.

The calf stopped at the sound of collision. Bird jolted down the slope of the shoulder and I tumbled from his back, down into the dark weeds. I felt my knee strike something hard, a rock maybe, or a culvert, then the numbness.

## 37

The black pickup roared by me. Teresa moved her hand in my direction but she wasn't smiling. I couldn't see

Lame Bull, but I knew that he too would be serious, even grim.

A faint movement in the air had started up, coming from the east, not enough to stir the cottonwood leaves, but enough to chill the sweat which ran down my rib cage. Dust from the road drifted toward the graveyard. There was one grave I hadn't looked at yet. It was marked with a white wooden cross just tall enough to stand above the weeds which grew up around it. Although I couldn't see it, there would be an unpainted wooden border around the grave. A circle of Styrofoam hung from the top point of the cross. From the bottom of the circle, pointing down, a piece of wire wrapped in green, and, below that, a faded paper flower barely visible in the weeds. There was no headstone, no name, no dates. My brother.

I put the tools away. I could smell rat poison in the shed. It had always smelled of rat poison.

I walked up to the house. The coffeepot on the back of the stove was still warm. A scent of perfume came from Teresa's bedroom. I closed the door, then poured a cup of coffee. I thought of Yellow Calf. The bottle of wine that Lame Bull and I had started on the night before was nearly full. I tucked it inside my shirt and walked down to the corral.

Bird did not fight me this time. He stood patiently as I cinched up the saddle and swung my leg over his back. The calf leaned against the far side of the loading chute. Beyond it, I could see its mother standing at the edge of the slough. She was looking at something on the other side.

The cottonwood leaves were beginning to flash as I

rode by the graveyard. I looked to the east. The clouds appeared to be moving up the valley, but they were still too far away to tell a direction. Overhead, a jet slid across the sky. I watched the silver glint until it glinted no more, leaving only a wispy tail to mark its course. A distant rumble caught up with us. Bird's ears flickered, but he plodded ahead down the dusty road.

I don't know how they figure it, old horse, but one year to me is worth four or five to you. That makes you over a hundred years, older than that old lady, and you're not only living, but carrying out your duties just like they trained you, beast of burden, though not a cow horse anymore.

I tied the reins together and looped them over the saddle horn. As I swung down, Bird shuddered and nuzzled me in the ribs. His nose brushed against the bottle under my shirt.

Now, old machine, I absolve you of your burden. You think I haven't noticed it. You don't show it. But that is the fault of your face. Your face was molded when you were born and hasn't changed in a hundred years. Your ears seem smaller now, but that is because your face has grown. You figure you have hidden this burden well. You have. But don't think I haven't seen it in your eyes those days when the clouds hide the sun and the cattle turn their asses to the wind. Those days your eyes tell me what you feel. It is the fault of the men who trained you to be a machine, to react to the pressure of a rein on your neck, spurs in your ribs, the sound of a voice. A cow horse. You weren't born that way; you were born to eat grass and drink slough water, to nip other horses in the flanks the way you do lagging bulls, to mount the mares. So they cut your balls off to make

you less temperamental, though I think they failed at
that. They haltered you, blindfolded you, waved gunny-
sacks at you and slapped you across the neck, the back
with leather. Finally they saddled you—didn't you try
to kick them when they reached under your belly for
the cinch?—and a man climbed on your back for the
first time. Only you can tell me how it felt to stand
quivering under the weight of that first man, dumb-
founded until—was it?—panic and anger began to
spread through your muscles and you erupted, rearing,
lunging, sunfishing around the corral until the man had
dug a furrow with his nose in the soft, flaky manure.
You must have felt cocky, proud, but the man—who
was it? surely not First Raise—the man climbed on your
back again and began to rake you with his spurs. Again
you reared and threw the man; again he dusted himself
off and climbed back on. Again and again, until you
were only crowhopping and running and swerving and
the man clung to the saddle horn and jerked your head
first one way, then the other, until you were confused
and half-blind with frustration. But you weren't
through. There was the final step—turn him out, somebody said, you heard it—and you raced through the
open gate, down the rutted road, your neck stretched
out as though you were after a carrot, and the man's
spurs dug deep in your ribs. You ran and ran for what
must have seemed like miles, not always following the
road, but always straight ahead, until you thought your
heart would explode against the terrible constriction of
its cage. It was this necessity, this knowledge of death,
that made you slow down to a stiff-legged trot, bearing
sideways, then a walk, and finally you found yourself
standing under a hot sun in the middle of a field of fox-

tail and speargrass, wheezing desperately to suck in the heavy air of a summer's afternoon. Not even the whirr of a sage hen as it lifted from a clump of rosebush ten feet away could make you lift that young tired head.

A cow horse.

I took a drink from the bottle of wine in an effort to relieve the tightness in my throat.

You have grown old, Bird, so old this sun consults your bones for weather reports. You are no longer a cow horse. No, don't think it was your fault—when that calf broke, you reacted as they trained you. I should compliment you on your eyes and your quickness. I didn't even see it break, then I felt your weight settle on your hind legs and the power . . .

I stopped to pick a burr from my pant leg, and I felt a dazzling rush in my head.

But I have seen you when the weather turns, when the sun is so high it no longer warms the earth but hangs pale above the chill wind, and the swift clouds, and dusk, the dusk, dusk . . .

"What use," I whispered, cried for no one in the world to hear, not even Bird, for no one but my soul, as though the words would rid it of the final burden of guilt, and I found myself a child again, the years shed as a snake sheds its skin, and I was standing over the awkward tangle of clothes and limbs. "What use, what use, what use . . ." and no one answered, not the body in the road, not the hawk in the sky or the beetle in the earth; no one answered. And the tears in the hot sun, in the wine, the dusk, the chilly wind of dusk, the sleet that began to fall as I knelt beside the body, the first sharp pain of my smashed knee, the sleet on my neck, the blood which dribbled from his nostrils, his mouth, the man who hurried back from his car, his terrible breath as he tried to wrestle me away from my brother's broken body.

# Part
# Four

## 38

"Hello," he said. "You are welcome."

"There are clouds in the east," I said. I could not look at him.

"I feel it, rain tonight maybe, tomorrow for sure, cats and dogs."

The breeze had picked up so that the willows on the irrigation ditch were gesturing in our direction.

"I see you wear shoes now. What's the meaning of this?" I pointed to a pair of rubber boots. His pants were tucked inside them.

"Rattlesnakes. For protection. This time of year they don't always warn you."

"They don't hear you," I said. "You're so quiet you take them by surprise."

"I found a skin beside my door this morning. I'm not taking any chances."

"I thought animals were your friends."

"Rattlesnakes are best left alone."

"Like you," I said.

"Could be."

I pumped some water into the enamel basin for Bird, then I loosened his cinch.

"I brought some wine." I held out the bottle.

"You are kind—you didn't have to."

"It's French," I said. "Made out of roses."

"My thirst is not so great as it once was. There was a time . . ." A gust of wind ruffled his fine white hair. "Let's have it."

I pressed the bottle into his hand. He held his head high, resting one hand on his chest, and drank greedily, his Adam's apple sliding up and down his throat as though it were attached to a piece of rubber. "And now, you," he said.

Yellow Calf squatted on the white skin of earth. I sat down on the platform on which the pump stood. Behind me, Bird sucked in the cool water.

"My grandmother died," I said. "We're going to bury her tomorrow."

He ran his paper fingers over the smooth rubber boots. He glanced in my direction, perhaps because he heard Bird's guts rumble. A small white cloud passed through the sun but he said nothing.

"She just stopped working. It was easy."

His knees cracked as he shifted his weight.

"We're going to bury her tomorrow. Maybe the priest from Harlem. He's a friend . . ."

He wasn't listening. Instead, his eyes were wandering

beyond the irrigation ditch to the hills and the muscled clouds above them.

Something about those eyes had prevented me from looking at him. It had seemed a violation of something personal and deep, as one feels when he comes upon a cow licking her newborn calf. But now, something else, his distance, made it all right to study his face, to see for the first time the black dots on his temples and the bridge of his nose, the ear lobes which sagged on either side of his head, and the bristles which grew on the edges of his jaw. Beneath his humped nose and above his chin, creases as well defined as cutbanks between prairie hills emptied into his mouth. Between his half-parted lips hung one snag, yellow and brown and worn-down, like that of an old horse. But it was his eyes, narrow beneath the loose skin of his lids, deep behind his cheekbones, that made one realize the old man's distance was permanent. It was behind those misty white eyes that gave off no light that he lived, a world as clean as the rustling willows, the bark of a fox or the odor of musk during mating season.

I wondered why First Raise had come so often to see him. Had he found a way to narrow that distance? I tried to remember that one snowy day he had brought me with him. I remembered Teresa and the old lady commenting on my father's judgment for taking me out on such a day; then riding behind him on the horse, laughing at the wet, falling snow. But I couldn't remember Yellow Calf or what the two men talked about.

"Did you know her at all?" I said.

Without turning his head, he said, "She was a young woman; I was just a youth."

"Then you did know her then."

"She was the youngest wife of Standing Bear."

I was reaching for the wine bottle. My hand stopped.

"He was a chief, a wise man—not like these conniving devils who run the agency today."

"How could you know Standing Bear? He was Blackfeet."

"We came from the mountains," he said.

"You're Blackfeet?"

"My people starved that winter; we all starved but they died. It was the cruelest winter. My folks died, one by one." He seemed to recollect this without emotion.

"But I thought you were Gros Ventre. I thought you were from around here."

"Many people starved that winter. We had to travel light—we were running from the soldiers—so we had few provisions. I remember, the day we entered this valley it began to snow and blizzard. We tried to hunt but the game refused to move. All winter long we looked for deer sign. I think we killed one deer. It was rare that we even jumped a porcupine. We snared a few rabbits but not enough . . ."

"You survived," I said.

"Yes, I was strong in those days." His voice was calm and monotonous.

"How about my grandmother? How did she survive?"

He pressed down on the toe of his rubber boot. It sprang back into shape.

"She said Standing Bear got killed that winter," I said.

"He led a party against the Gros Ventres. They had meat. I was too young. I remember the men when they returned to camp—it was dark but you could see the white air from their horses' nostrils. We all stood waiting, for we were sure they would bring meat. But they brought Standing Bear's body instead. It was a bad time."

I tapped Yellow Calf's knee with the bottle. He drank, then wiped his lips on his shirt sleeve.

"It was then that we knew our medicine had gone bad. We had wintered some hard times before, winters were always hard, but seeing Standing Bear's body made us realize that we were being punished for having left our home. The people resolved that as soon as spring came we would go home, soldiers or not."

"But you stayed," I said. "Why?"

He drew an arc with his hand, palm down, taking in the bend of the river behind his house. It was filled with tall cottonwoods, most of them dead, with tangles of brush and wild rose around their trunks. The land sloped down from where we were sitting so that the bend was not much higher than the river itself.

"This was where we camped. It was not grown over then, only the cottonwoods were standing. But the willows were thick then, all around to provide a shelter. We camped very close together to take advantage of this situation. Sometimes in winter, when the wind has packed the snow and blown the clouds away, I can still hear the muttering of the people in their tepees. It was a very bad time."

"And your family starved . . ."

"My father died of something else, a sickness, pneumonia maybe. I had four sisters. They were among the first to go. My mother hung on for a little while but soon she went. Many starved."

"But if the people went back in the spring, why did you stay?"

"My people were here."

"And the old—my grandmother stayed too," I said.

"Yes. Being a widow is not easy work, especially when your husband had other wives. She was the youngest. She was considered quite beautiful in those days."

"But why did she stay?"

He did not answer right away. He busied himself scraping a star in the tough skin of earth. He drew a circle around it and made marks around it as a child draws the sun. Then he scraped it away with the end of his stick and raised his face into the thickening wind. "You must understand how people think in desperate times. When their bellies are full, they can afford to be happy and generous with each other—the meat is shared, the women work and gossip, men gamble—it's a good time and you do not see things clearly. There is no need. But when the pot is empty and your guts are tight in your belly, you begin to look around. The hunger sharpens your eye."

"But why her?"

"She had not been with us more than a month or two, maybe three. You must understand the thinking. In that time the soldiers came, the people had to leave their home up near the mountains, then the starvation and the death of their leader. She had brought them bad medicine."

"But you—you don't think that."

"It was apparent," he said.

"It was bad luck; the people grew angry because their luck was bad," I said.

"It was medicine."

I looked at his eyes. "She said it was because of her beauty."

"I believe it was that too. When Standing Bear was

alive, they had to accept her. In fact, they were proud
to have such beauty—you know how it is, even if it isn't
yours." His lips trembled into what could have been a
smile.

"But when he died, her beauty worked against her,"
I said.

"That's true, but it was more than that. When you
are starving, you look for signs. Each event becomes big
in your mind. His death was the final proof that they
were cursed. The medicine man, Fish, interpreted the
signs. They looked at your grandmother and realized
that she had brought despair and death. And her
beauty—it was as if her beauty made a mockery of their
situation."

"They can't have believed this . . ."

"It wasn't a question of belief, it was the way things
were," he said. "The day Standing Bear was laid to rest,
the women walked away. Even his other wives gave her
the silent treatment. It took the men longer—men are
not sensitive. They considered her the widow of a chief
and treated her with respect. But soon, as it must be,
they began to notice the hatred in their women's eyes,
the coolness with which they were treated if they
brought your grandmother a rabbit leg or a piece of
fire in the morning. And they became ashamed of themselves for associating with the young widow and left
her to herself."

I was staring at the bottle on the ground before me.
I tried to understand the medicine, the power that
directed the people to single out a young woman, to
leave her to fend for herself in the middle of a cruel
winter. I tried to understand the thinking, the hatred
of the women, the shame of the men. Starvation. I didn't

know it. I couldn't understand the medicine, her beauty.

"What happened to her?"

"She lived the rest of the winter by herself."

"How could she survive alone?"

He shifted his weight and dug his stick into the earth. He seemed uncomfortable. Perhaps he was recalling things he didn't want to or he felt that he had gone too far. He seemed to have lost his distance, but he went on: "She didn't really leave. It was the dead of winter. To leave the camp would have meant a sure death, but there were tepees on the edge, empty—many were empty then."

"What did she do for food?"

"What did any of us do? We waited for spring. Spring came, we hunted—the deer were weak and easy to kill."

"But she couldn't hunt, could she?" It seemed important for me to know what she did for food. No woman, no man could live a winter like that alone without something.

As I watched Yellow Calf dig at the earth I remembered how the old lady had ended her story of the journey of Standing Bear's band.

There had been great confusion that spring. Should the people stay in this land of the Gros Ventres, should they go directly south to the nearest buffalo herd, or should they go back to the country west of here, their home up near the mountains? The few old people left were in favor of this last direction because they wanted to die in familiar surroundings, but the younger ones were divided as to whether they should stay put until they got stronger or head for the buffalo ranges to the south. They rejected the idea of going home because the soldiers were there. Many of them had encountered

the Long Knives before, and they knew that in their con-
dition they wouldn't have a chance. There was much
confusion, many decisions and indecisions, hostility.

Finally it was the soldiers from Fort Assiniboine who
took the choice away from the people. They rode down
one late-spring day, gathered up the survivors and drove
them west to the newly created Blackfeet Reservation.
Because they didn't care to take her with them, the
people apparently didn't mention her to the soldiers, and
because she had left the band when the weather
warmed and lived a distance away, the soldiers didn't
question her. They assumed she was a Gros Ventre.

A gust of wind rattled the willows. The clouds
towered white against the sky, but I could see their
black underbellies as they floated toward us.

The old lady had ended her story with the image of
the people being driven "like cows" to their reservation.
It was a strange triumph and I understood it. But why
hadn't she spoken of Yellow Calf? Why hadn't she
mentioned that he was a member of that band of
Blackfeet and had, like herself, stayed behind?

A swirl of dust skittered across the earth's skin.

"You say you were just a youth that winter—how
old?" I said.

He stopped digging. "That first winter, my folks all
died then."

But I was not to be put off. "How old?"

"It slips my mind," he said. "When one is blind and
old he loses track of the years."

"You must have some idea."

"When one is blind . . ."

"Ten? Twelve? Fifteen?"

". . . and old, he no longer follows the cycles of the

years. He knows each season in its place because he can feel it, but time becomes a procession. Time feeds upon itself and grows fat." A mosquito took shelter in the hollow of his cheek, but he didn't notice. He had attained that distance. "To an old dog like myself, the only cycle begins with birth and ends in death. This is the only cycle I know."

I thought of the calendar I had seen in his shack on my previous visit. It was dated 1936. He must have been able to see then. He had been blind for over thirty years, but if he was as old as I thought, he had lived out a lifetime before. He had lived a life without being blind. He had followed the calendar, the years, time—

I thought for a moment.

Bird farted.

And it came to me, as though it were riding one moment of the gusting wind, as though Bird had had it in him all the time and had passed it to me in that one instant of corruption.

"Listen, old man," I said. "It was you—you were old enough to hunt!"

But his white eyes were kneading the clouds.

I began to laugh, at first quietly, with neither bitterness nor humor. It was the laughter of one who understands a moment in his life, of one who has been let in on the secret through luck and circumstance. "You . . . you're the one." I laughed, as the secret unfolded itself. "The only one . . . you, her hunter . . ." And the wave behind my eyes broke.

Yellow Calf still looked off toward the east as though the wind could wash the wrinkles from his face. But the corners of his eyes wrinkled even more as his mouth fell open. Through my tears I could see his Adam's apple jerk.

"The only one," I whispered, and the old man's head dropped between his knees. His back shook, the bony shoulders squared and hunched like the folded wings of a hawk.

"And the half-breed, Doagie!" But the laughter again racked my throat. *He wasn't Teresa's father; it was you, Yellow Calf, the hunter!*

He turned to the sound of my laughter. His face was distorted so that the single snag seemed the only recognizable feature of the man I had come to visit. His eyes hid themselves behind the high cheekbones. His mouth had become the rubbery sneer of a jack-o'-lantern.

And so we shared this secret in the presence of ghosts, in wind that called forth the muttering tepees, the blowing snow, the white air of the horses' nostrils. The cottonwoods behind us, their dead white branches angling to the threatening clouds, sheltered these ghosts as they had sheltered the camp that winter. But there were others, so many others.

Yellow Calf stood, his hands in his pockets, suddenly withdrawn and polite. I pressed what remained of the bottle of wine into his hand. "Thank you," he said.

"You must come visit me sometime," I said.

"You are kind."

I tightened the cinch around Bird's belly. "I'll think about you," I said.

"You'd better hurry," he said. "It's coming."

I picked up the reins and led Bird to the rotting plank bridge across the irrigation ditch.

He lifted his hand.

## 39

Bird held his head high as he trotted down the fence line. He was anxious to get home. He was in a hurry to have a good pee and a good roll in the manure. Since growing old, he had lost his grace. With each step, I felt the leather of the saddle rub against my thighs.

It was a good time for odor. Alfalfa, sweet and dusty, came with the wind, above it the smell of rain. The old man would be lifting his nose to this odor, thinking of other things, of those days he stood by the widow when everyone else had failed her. So much distance between them, and yet they lived only three miles apart. But what created this distance? And what made me think that he was Teresa's father? After all, twenty-five years had passed between the time he had become my grandmother's hunter and Teresa's birth. They could have parted at any time. But he was the one. I knew that. The answer had come to me as if by instinct, sitting on the pump platform, watching his silent laughter, as though it was his blood in my veins that had told me.

I tried to imagine what it must have been like, the two of them, hunter and widow. If I was right about Yellow Calf's age, there couldn't have been more than four or five years separating them. If she was not yet twenty, he must have been fifteen or sixteen. Old enough to hunt, but what about the other? Could he have been more than hunter then, or did that come later? It seemed likely that they had never lived together (except perhaps that first winter out of need). There had never been any talk, none that I heard. The woman who had told me about Doagie had implied that he hadn't been Teresa's father. She hadn't mentioned Yellow Calf.

So for years the three miles must have been as close as an early morning walk down this path I was now riding. The fence hadn't been here in the beginning, nor the odor of alfalfa. But the other things, the cotton-woods and willows, the open spaces of the valley, the hills to the south, the Little Rockies, had all been here then; none had changed. Bird lifted his head and whinnied. He had settled into a gait that would have been a dance in his younger days. It was only the thudding of his hooves and the saddle rubbing against my thighs that gave him away. So for years the old man had made this trip; but could it have been twenty-five? Twenty-five years without living together, twenty-five years of an affair so solemn and secretive it had not even been rumored?

Again I thought of the time First Raise had taken me to see the old man. Again I felt the cold canvas of his coat as I clung to him, the steady clopping of the horse's hooves on the frozen path growing quieter as the wet snow began to pile up. I remembered the flour sack filled with frozen deer meat hanging from the saddle horn, and First Raise getting down to open the gate, then peeing what he said was my name in the snow. But I couldn't remember being at the shack. I couldn't remember Yellow Calf.

Yet I had felt it then, that feeling of event. Perhaps it was the distance, those three new miles, that I felt, or perhaps I had felt something of that other distance; but the event of distance was as vivid to me as the cold canvas of First Raise's coat against my cheek. He must have known then what I had just discovered. Although he told me nothing of it up to the day he died, he had taken me that snowy day to see my grandfather.

## 40

A glint of sunlight caught my eye. A car was pulling off the highway onto our road. It was too far away to recognize. It looked like a dark beetle lumbering slowly over the bumps and ruts of the dusty tracks. I had reached the gate but I didn't get down. Bird pawed the ground and looked off toward the ranch. From this angle only the slough and corral were visible. Bird studied them. The buildings were hidden behind a rise in the road.

The clouds were now directly overhead, but the sun to the west was still glaring hot. The wind had died down to a steady breeze. The rain was very close.

It was Ferdinand Horn and his wife. As the dark green Hudson hit the stretch of raised road between the alfalfa fields, he honked the horn as if I had planned to disappear. He leaned out his window and waved. "Hello there, partner," he called. He turned off the motor and the car coasted to a stop. He looked up at me. "We just stopped to offer our condolences."

"What?"

Ferdinand Horn's wife leaned forward on the seat and looked up through the windshield. She had a pained look.

"Oh, the old lady!" It was strange, but I had forgotten that she was dead.

"She was a fine woman," Ferdinand Horn said. He gazed at the alfalfa field out his window.

"Teresa and Lame Bull went to Harlem to get her. They probably won't get back before dark."

"We saw them. We just came from there," he said. He seemed to be measuring the field. "A lovely woman."

Ferdinand Horn's wife stared at me through her turquoise-frame glasses. She had cocked her head to get a better look. It must have been uncomfortable.

"We're going to bury her tomorrow," I said.

"The hell you say."

"We're not doing anything fancy. You could probably come if you want to." I didn't know exactly how Teresa would act at the funeral.

"That's an idea." He turned to his wife. She nodded, still looking up through the windshield. "Oh hell, where's my manners." He fumbled in a paper sack between them. He punched two holes in the bottom of a can of beer. It had a pop-top on top. He handed it to me.

I took a sip, then a swallow, and another. The wine had left my mouth dry, and the beer was good and colder than I expected. "Jesus," I gasped. "That really hits the spot."

"I don't know what's wrong with me. What the hell are you doing on that damn plug?"

"I was just riding around. I visited Yellow Calf for a minute."

"No kidding? I thought he was dead." He looked at the field again. "How is he anyway?"

"He seems to be okay, living to the best of his ability," I said.

"You know, my cousin Louie used to bring him commodities when he worked for Reclamation. He used to regulate that head gate back by Yellow Calf's, and he'd bring him groceries. But hell, that was ten years ago— hell, twenty!"

I hadn't thought of that aspect. How did he eat now? "Maybe the new man brings him food," I said.

"He's kind of goofy, you know."

"The new man?"

"Yellow Calf."

Ferdinand Horn's wife pushed her glasses up, then wrinkled her nose to keep them there. She was holding a can of grape pop in her lap. She had wrapped a light blue hankie around it to keep her hand from getting cold or sticky.

"You have a low spot in that corner over there."

I followed his finger to an area of the field filled with slough grass and foxtail.

"Did you find her?" The muffled voice brought me back to the car.

"We're going to bury her tomorrow," I said.

"No, no," she shrieked, and hit Ferdinand Horn on the chest. "Your wife!" She hadn't taken her eyes off me. "Your wife!"

It was a stab in the heart. "I saw her . . . in Havre," I said.

"Well?"

"In Gable's . . ."

She leaned forward and toward Ferdinand Horn. Her upper lip lifted over her small brown teeth. "Was that white man with her?"

"No, she was all alone this time."

"I'll bet—"

"How many bales you get off this piece?"

"I'll bet she was all alone. As if a girl like that could

ever be alone." She looked up like a muskrat through the thin ice of the windshield.

"We just came by to offer our condolences."

"Don't try to change the subject," she said, slapping Ferdinand Horn on the arm. "Did you bring her back?"

"Yes," I said. "She's in at the house now. Do you want to see her?"

"You mean you brought her back?" She sounded disappointed.

"You want to see her?"

"Did you get your gun back?" Ferdinand Horn was now looking at me.

"Yes. Do you want to see her?"

"Okay, sure, for a minute," he said.

His wife fell back against the seat. She was wearing the same wrinkled print dress she had worn the time before. Her thighs were spread beneath the bright butterflies. I couldn't see her face.

"We're late enough," she said.

"Well, just for a minute," Ferdinand Horn said.

"We just came by to offer our condolences."

Ferdinand Horn seemed puzzled. He turned toward her. Her thighs tightened. He looked up at me. Then he started the car. "How many bales you get off this piece?" he said.

## 41

As Bird and I rounded the bend of the slough, I could hear the calf bawling. It was almost feeding time. We passed the graveyard with its fresh dirt now turning

165

tan beneath the rolling clouds. Bird loped straight for the corral, his ears forward and his legs stiffened. I could feel the tension in his body. I thought it was because of the storm which threatened to break at any time, but as we neared the corral, Bird pulled up short and glanced in the direction of the slough. It was the calf's mother. She was lying on her side, up to her chest in the mud. Her good eye was rimmed white and her tongue lolled from the side of her mouth. When she saw us, she made an effort to free herself, as though we had come to encourage her. Her back humped forward as her shoulders strained against the sucking mud. She switched her tail and a thin stream of crap ran down her backside.

Bird whinnied, then dropped his head, waiting for me to get down and open the gate. He had lost interest.

I wanted to ignore her. I wanted to go away, to let her drown in her own stupidity, attended only by clouds and the coming rain. If I turned away now, I thought, if I turned away—my hands trembled but did nothing. She had earned this fate by being stupid, and now no one could help her. Who would want to? As she stared at me, I saw beyond the immediate panic that hatred, that crazy hatred that made me aware of a quick hatred in my own heart. Her horns seemed tipped with blood, the dark blood of catastrophe. The muck slid down around her ears as she lowered her head, the air from her nostrils blowing puddles in the mud. I had seen her before, the image of catastrophe, the same hateful eye, the long curving horns, the wild-eyed spinster leading the cows down the hill into the valley. Stupid, stupid cow, hateful in her stupidity. She let out a long, bubbling call. I continued to glance at her, but now, as though energy, or even life, had gone out of her, she rolled her head to one side, half submerged in the mud, her one eye staring wildly at the clouds.

Stupid, stupid—

I slid down, threw open the corral gate and ran to the horse shed. The soft flaky manure cushioned the jolt of my bad leg. A rope hung from a nail driven into a two-by-four. I snatched it down and ran back to the gate. Bird was just sauntering through. I half led, half dragged him down to the edge of the slough. He seemed offended that I should ask this task of him. He tried to look around toward the pasture behind the corral. The red horse was watching us over the top pole, but there was no time to exchange horses. Already the cow lay motionless on her side.

I tied one end of the rope to the saddle horn to keep Bird from walking away, then threw open the loop to fit over the cow's head. But she would not lift it. I yelled and threw mud toward her, but she made no effort. My scalp began to sweat. A chilly breeze blew through my hair as I twirled the loop above my head. I tried for her horn but it was pointing forward toward me and the loop slid off. Again and again I threw for the horn, but the loop had nothing to tighten against. Each time I expected her to raise her head in response to the loop landing roughly against her neck and head, but she lay still. She must be dead, I thought, but the tiny bubbles around her nostrils continued to fizz. Then I was in the mud, up to my knees, wading out to the cow. With each step, the mud closed around my leg, then the heavy suck as I pulled the other free. My eyes fixed themselves on the bubbles and I prayed for them to stop so I could turn back, but the frothy mass continued to expand and move as though it were life itself. I was in up to my crotch, no longer able to lift my legs, able only to slide them through the greasy mire. The two or three inches of stagnant water sent the smell of dead things through my body. It was too late, it was taking too long—by leaning forward I could almost reach the cow's horn. One more step, the bubbles weren't moving, and I did clutch the horn, pulling myself toward her. She tried to lift her head, but the mud sucked it back down. Her open mouth, filling with slime, looked as pink as a baby mouse against the green and black. The wild eye, now trying to focus on me, was streaked with the red threads of panic.

By lifting on her horn, I managed to raise her head enough to slide the loop underneath, the mud now working to my advantage. I tightened up and yelled to Bird, at the same time pulling the rope against the saddle horn. The old horse shook his shoulders and backed up. He reared a few inches off the ground, as though the pressure of the rope had reminded him of those years spent as a cow horse. But the weight of the cow and mud began to pull the saddle forward, the back end lifting away from his body. It wouldn't hold. I gripped the taut rope and pulled myself up and out of the mud. I began to move hand over hand back toward the bank. Something had gone wrong with my knee; it wouldn't bend. I tried to arch my toes to keep my shoe from being pulled off, but there was no response. My whole leg was dead. The muscles in my arms knotted, but I continued to pull myself along the rope until I reached the edge of the bank. I lay there a moment, exhausted, then tried to get up but my arms wouldn't move. It was a dream. I couldn't move my arms. They lay at my sides, palms up, limp, as though they belonged to another body. I bent my good knee up under me, using my shoulders and chin as leverage.

Once again I yelled at Bird, but he would not come, would not slack up on the rope. I swore at him, coaxed him, reasoned with him, but I must have looked foolish to him, my ass in the air and the sweat running from my scalp.

Goddamn you, Bird, goddamn you. Goddamn Ferdinand Horn, why didn't you come in, together we could have gotten this damn cow out, why hadn't I ignored her? Goddamn your wife with her stupid turquoise glasses, stupid grape pop, your stupid car. Lame Bull! It was his cow, he had married this cow, why wasn't he here? Off riding around, playing the role, goddamn big-time operator, can't trust him, can't trust any of these damn idiots, damn Indians. Slack up, you asshole! Slack up! You want to strangle her? That's okay with me; she means nothing to me. What did I do to deserve this? Goddamn that Ferdinand Horn! Ah, Teresa, you made a terrible mistake. Your husband, your friends, your son, all worthless, none of them worth a shit. Slack up, you sonofabitch! Your mother dead, your father—you don't even know, what do you think of that? A joke, can't you see? Lame Bull! The biggest joke—can't you see that he's a joke, a joker playing a joke on you? Were you taken for a ride! Just like the rest of us, this country, all of us taken for a ride. Slack up, slack up! This greedy stupid country—

My arms began to tingle as they tried to wake up. I moved my fingers. They moved. My neck ached but the strength was returning. I crouched and spent the next few minutes planning my new life. Finally I was able to push myself from the ground and stand on my good leg. I put my weight on the other. The bones seemed to be wedged together, but it didn't hurt. I hobbled over to Bird. He raised his head and nodded wildly. As I touched his shoulder, he shied back even further.

"Here, you old sonofabitch," I said. "Do you want to defeat our purpose?"

He nodded his agreement. I hit the rope with the edge of my hand. I hit it again. He let off, dancing forward, the muscles in his shoulders working beneath the soft white hair. I looked back at the cow. She was standing up in the mud, her head, half of it black, straight up like a swimming water snake. I snapped the rope out toward her, but she didn't move. Her eyes were wild, a glaze beginning to form in them. The noose was still tight around her neck.

As I climbed aboard the horse, I noticed for the first time that it was raining. What I thought was sweat running through my scalp had been rain all along. I snapped the rope again, arcing a curve away from me toward the cow. This time the noose did loosen up. She seemed surprised. A loud gasp, as harsh as a dog's bark, came from her throat. As though that were her signal for a final death struggle, she went into action, humping her back, bawling, straining against the sucking mud. Bird tightened up on the rope and began to back away. The saddle came forward; I turned him so that he was headed away from the slough.

The rain was coming hard now, the big drops stinging the back of my neck and splattering into the dusty earth. A magpie, light and silent, flew overhead, then lit on a fence post beside the loading chute. He ruffled his sleek feathers, then squatted to watch.

The rope began to hum in the gathering wind, but the cow was coming, flailing her front legs out of the mud. Bird slipped once and almost went down, doing a strange dance, rolling quickly from side to side, but he regained his balance and continued to pull and the cow continued to come. I took another dally around the saddle horn and clung to the end of the rope. I slapped him on the shoulder. Somewhere in my mind I could hear the deep rumble of thunder, or maybe it was the rumble of energy, the rumble of guts—it didn't matter. There was only me, a white horse and a cow. The pressure of the rope against my thigh felt right. I sat to one side in the saddle, standing in the right stirrup, studying the rough strands of hemp against the pant leg. The cow had quit struggling and was now sliding slowly through the greasy mud. Her head pointed up into the rain, but her eyes had lost that wild glare. She seemed to understand this necessary inconvenience.

It was all so smooth and natural I didn't notice that Bird had begun to slip in the rain-slick dirt. He turned sideways in an attempt to get more traction. He lowered his rump and raised his head. He lowered his head again so that he was stretched low to the ground. I leaned forward until I could smell the sweet warmth of his wet mane. Then I felt the furious digging of hooves, and I realized that he was about to go down. Before I could react, he whirled around, his front legs striking out at the air. His hind legs went out from under him. It was only the weight of the cow on the end of the rope that kept him from falling over backwards on top of me. His large white butt thumped the ground in front of me, he tottered for an instant, then he fell forward and it was quiet.

## 42

A flash of lightning to the south of me. I couldn't or wouldn't turn my head. I felt my back begin to stiffen. I didn't know if it was because of the fall or the damp, but I wasn't uncomfortable. The stiffness provided a reason for not moving. I saw the flash in the corner of my eye, as though it were mirrored countless times in the countless raindrops that fell on my face.

I wondered if Mose and First Raise were comfortable. They were the only ones I really loved, I thought, the only ones who were good to be with. At least the rain wouldn't bother them. But they would probably like it; they were that way, good to be with, even on a rainy day.

I heard Bird grunt twice as he tried to heave himself upright, but I couldn't find the energy to look at him. The magpie must have flown closer, for his metallic *awk! awk!* was almost conversational. The cow down in the slough had stopped gurgling. Her calf called once, a soft drone which ended on a quizzical high note. Then it was silent again.

Some people, I thought, will never know how pleasant it is to be distant in a clean rain, the driving rain of a summer storm. It's not like you'd expect, nothing like you'd expect.

# Epilogue

We buried the old lady the next day. The priest from
Harlem, of course, couldn't make it. So there were the
four of us—Teresa, Lame Bull, me and my grandmother. I hadn't told them about Ferdinand Horn and
his wife, but they wouldn't show up anyway. I had to
admit that Lame Bull looked pretty good. The buttons
on his shiny green suit looked like they were made of
wood. Although his crotch hung a little low, the pants
were the latest style. Teresa had shortened the legs
that morning, a makeshift job, having only had time to
tack the original cuffs up inside the pant legs. His fancy
boots with the walking heels peeked out from beneath
the new cuffs. His shirt, tie, handkerchief and belt were
various shades of green and red to match the suit. He

smelled of Wildroot and after-shave lotion. I felt seedy standing beside him. I was wearing a suit that had belonged to my father. I hadn't known it existed until an hour before the funeral. It was made out of a cream-colored wool with brown threads running through it. The collar and cuffs itched in the noonday heat, but the pant legs were wide enough so that if I stood just right I didn't touch them, except for my knee which was swollen up. It still didn't hurt. The necktie, which I had loosened, had also belonged to my father. It was silk with a picture of two mallards flying over a stand of cattails.

Teresa wore a black coat, black high heels, and a black cupcake hat. A black net extended down from it to cover her eyes and nose. It stopped just above her upper lip. She had painted her stern lips a bright red. Once again she was big and handsome—except for her legs. They appeared to be a little skinny, but it must have been the dress. I wasn't used to seeing her legs.

The old lady wore a shiny orange coffin with flecks of black ingrained beneath the surface. It had been sealed up in Harlem, so we never did find out what kind of makeup job the undertaker had done on her.

The hole was too short, but we didn't discover this until we had the coffin halfway down. One end went down easily enough, but the other stuck against the wall. Teresa wanted us to take it out because she was sure that it was the head that was lower than the feet. Lame Bull lowered himself into the grave and jumped up and down on the high end. It went down a bit more, enough to look respectable. Teresa didn't say anything, so he leaped out of the hole, a little too quickly. He wiped his forehead with the pale green handkerchief.

"Well," he said. It was a question. He looked at me and I looked off toward the slough, fingering the tobacco pouch.

Teresa began to moan. She wavered back and forth as though the heat were getting to her.

"What do you think, pal?"

The air was heavy with yesterday's rain. It would probably be good for fishing.

"I suppose me being the head of the family, it's up to me to say a few words about our beloved relative and friend."

Teresa moaned.

Lame Bull clasped his hands in front of him. "Well," he said. "Here lies a simple woman . . . who devoted herself to . . . rocking . . and not a bad word about anybody . . ."

I shifted my weight to my bad leg. It was like standing on tree stump.

"Not the best mother in the world . . ."

Teresa moaned louder.

". . . but a good mother, notwithstanding . . ."

I would have to go to the agency and see the doctor. I knew that he would try to send me down to Great Falls to have it operated on. But I couldn't do it. I'd tell him that. I would end up in bed for a year. By that time the girl who had stolen my gun and electric razor would have forgotten me.

Teresa fell to her knees.

". . . who could take it and dish it out . . ."

Next time I'd do it right. Buy her a couple of crèmes de menthe, maybe offer to marry her on the spot.

"... who never gave anybody any crap ..."

The red horse down in the corral whinnied. He probably missed old Bird.

I threw the pouch into the grave.

Typography and binding design by Christine Aulicino
Jacket design by Robert Aulicino
Edited by Theodore Solotaroff
Program editor: Douglas H. Latimer
Production by Karen Whitney
Composed, printed, and bound by
The Haddon Craftsmen, Inc.,
Scranton, Pennsylvania.